KV-512-109

# THE CLIENTS OF
# MISS MAY

Also by DENNIS BARKER

# ANGUS LIBRARIES

38046 01 002769 5

**Angus** Council

www.angus.gov.uk/libraries

**Return to.................. CARNOUSTIE ........... Library**

Please return/renew this item by the last date shown
Items may also be renewed by phone or online

0 2 JUN 2010
2 1 JUN 2010
1 5 DEC 2010
2 5 APR 2012
- 3 FEB 2020

WITHDRAWN FROM STOCK

FEB 10 B T

# The Clients of Miss May

DENNIS BARKER

QUARTET

First published in 2008 by
Quartet Books Limited
A member of the Namara Group
27 Goodge Street, London W1T 2LD

Copyright © Dennis Barker 2008

The right of Dennis Barker to be identified
as the author of this work has been asserted
by him in accordance with the
Copyright, Designs and Patents Act, 1988

All rights reserved.
No part of this book may be reproduced in
any form or by any means without prior
written permission from the publisher

A catalogue record for this book
is available from the British Library

ISBN    978 0 7043 7141 5

Typeset by Antony Gray
Printed and bound in Great Britain by
T J International Ltd, Padstow, Cornwall

*Part One*

# 1

'She appears to fancy you, Sandy – decidedly so,' said Tom Webster, reaching towards him with the whisky bottle.

'You're having me on!' said Sandy Britton, waving the bottle away and covering his glass with his hand. 'It's the sort of thing bar girls must say all the time.'

'I know her. It's real enough for me to be slightly irritated, old son. Or hadn't you noticed that either?'

'Your fault for praising me up like that in the first place, Tom. Anyway you've got me more than half pissed as usual and I've got to tear myself away from your very nice apartment and drinks and get back to the ship before I get put in irons or whatever they do to you now if you don't turn up on time.'

'Sub-Lieutenant Britton does his duty to HMS *War Lion* and the British Empire! Except – hadn't you noticed that either? – there is no empire, or won't be next year, to be precise. It's 1996, chum: next year we'll no longer be lords and masters in Hong Kong. Visits like this will be few and far between, even if the navy comes here at all. She likes you. You like her – I could see that, too. Take what you can when you can. It's the essence of wisdom, as you'll discover one day in the – dare one hope? – not too distant future.'

'You're as pissed as I am. Wisdom? In the navy, they'd call that low bloody opportunism.'

'Dear, dear! Let us sing Rule Britannia or at least pray for all idealists on land and sea.'

'Tom, is there anything at all you take seriously?'

'If you notice anything, tell me at once and I'll soon put a stop to it.'

May Fong – the European form of address she still preferred – had been in the bathroom for at least ten awkward minutes. Perhaps she had sensed the slightest tension between Tom Webster, her regular client and her regular host at the apartment distantly overlooking Victoria Harbour, and his much younger guest. It could have been her way of leaving them alone together to sort it out.

Sandy Britton's cheeks were burning with embarrassment as well as the stifling heat. He felt too hot to sort anything out. The windows that led to the small balcony of the eighth floor Kennedy Road apartment were open, which meant the place was hotter and stickier than it would have been had the air conditioning been given a chance. Tom said he liked to feel in touch with the world. The fax machine on the black lacquer occasional table, the telephone answering machine on the bamboo dining table and the short wave radio on the drinks tray indicated this declaration, at any rate, was sincere. There was very little, even for a divorced man, in the way of domestic comforts in the apartment, only evidence of his close marriage to the South East Asia News and Views Agency and Famous Grouse scotch. His cigarette lighter was a disposable one. The spare room was even more spartan than the rest of the apartment, with nothing in it except a double bed and piles of books, newspapers and magazines against the walls.

May Fong, as Tom had assured his friend, was as discreet as she was beautiful. No doubt she would continue to be discreet after the British Crown Lease of the crucial Kowloon and New Territories north of Hong Kong Isand expired and the Chinese took over. She had a smooth ivory oval face, elegantly long for a Chinese; her slender waist accentuated her full breasts and well-rounded hips. She was twenty and to Western eyes looked even younger.

She had come to Tom Webster's apartment every Friday evening for the past six months, punctually at nine, dressed almost primly in dark cotton frocks or pyjama suits. Tonight she was wearing flared black slacks and a short oatmeal safari jacket with a flared hem that made it look vaguely balletic. She always left equally punctually at midnight, the roll of Hong Kong dollar notes tucked uncounted into her black patent leather handbag. She went straight back to Madam Cat's Hot Cat Club in the better part of the Wanchai club and bar district, where she took her place on one of the tall red simulated leather bar stools and waited for other regular or casual clients; finally, not long before dawn, going home to her tenement room just round the corner.

Only once had Tom Webster paid her to stay all night. It was his birthday and the first anniversary of his divorce and he had felt lonely. That was the night she had told him about her mother, whose whereabouts in China she now did not know. She spoke of her brother in Hong Kong who was in police custody again; apparently he often fell foul of the authorities in one way or another. She had also let slip something about a younger sister, but then almost immediately had became evasive, claiming, when he questioned her, that he had mis-understood her, that she had no younger sister. He had never wanted to repeat that night's experience. It wasn't that it had cost him a lot of money, though it had. He didn't want to get too close; not to anyone.

Pushing such memories firmly to the back of his mind, Tom Webster said in his usual joshing tone of voice: 'I think it must be the fair hair. That and the unworldly air of innocence and rectitude. For heaven's sake don't tell her you were once a journalist.' He looked at Sandy closely over the top of his whisky glass.

Sandy was not amused. His close-cropped hair was wet rather than merely damp. At only medium height and with a few more inches round the waist than he should have had at twenty-something, he had never imagined himself as attractive to anybody. He had caught sight of his face in the misted-over bamboo framed mirror in the bathroom and his blue eyes looked bleary. He had knocked over the tumbler on the washbasin when drying his hands; he had always been prone to physical clumsiness.

'I always draw a veil over Fleet Street,' he said, forming his words with care since his tongue did not seem to be as securely under the control of his mind as it had been when he had entered the apartment. 'The top brass say they excuse it only because I was young at the time. I get my leg pulled about it.'

'Young? Despite my best efforts at your education in the old black art of news agency journalism, you were scarcely born.'

'I wasn't as hopeless as all that.'

'If you were, old son, it was only because you were too good, or at least too high-minded, for the job . . . You're not feeling ill, are you?'

'Is it always as damp as this in Hong Kong?'

'A hundred years ago, you were hardly in the place for five minutes before you went down with some fever or other. You could count on it. People died like flies. It's better than that now.'

'Slightly,' said Sandy, undoing another button of his white shirt. His chest was all but hairless and he hastily did the button up again before Tom found something else out of which he could take the piss.

There was a smear of condensation over practically everything in the apartment, including the bamboo furniture which

Tom made no secret of buying as a substandard job-lot at one of the little workshops in the Queens Road, straight down Kennedy Road and turn left towards the screeching trams and glaring neon signs of Central and Wanchai. The living room was small, its walls painted white, the french window to the balcony thrown open despite the fact it all but completely nullified the air conditioning. Tom said he liked to hear what was going on. The humidity, inside and out, was approaching one hundred per cent, at which point nothing at all would remain dry.

Tom Webster swept his receding hair back over his bald patch, gasped for air and poured himself another whisky. He was in his forties and knew he looked older. His once hand-some face was now decorated with broken blood vessels. He was wearing white slacks, a yellow shirt open to the navel and revealing matted black hairs. He wore the type of sandals which stayed on by courtesy of a single leather thong. He had taken off his black-faced Rolex and laid it beside the fax machine. It wasn't the weather for being overweight and over forty; he envied his twenty-odd friend as much for his slimmer waistline as for his air of innocence, both of which appealed to him as much now as they had done in that dim and distant past (was it only five years or so?) when he had been the so-called chief reporter on that small news and features agency in a dying or dead Fleet Street and Sandy had turned up as an almost totally unsuitable junior. He had failed to bring back from the widow a photograph of her just-killed pilot husband, explaining that the weeping woman had claimed it was her only one. The whole office had erupted into laughter over that.

Sandy had left because the job obviously hadn't suited him; Tom Webster had left a little later to join the South East Asia News and Views Agency in Hong Kong when his never con-spicuous marriage had at last fallen apart. He said he hadn't in any case fancied a move to Canary Wharf or the Isle of Dogs to keep close to his newspaper and magazine clients. Now Sandy was, more suitably, in the Royal Navy and miles from home; and here they both were again, this time in the Far East, getting pissed as they had sometimes done in the remaining picturesque pubs of Fleet Street.

'You'd be a fool not to have her, Sandy. She can be quite miraculous at it, I assure you. Those nipples like walnuts. Those thighs . . . Christ, you're actually blushing. I didn't think people did that any more.'

'I'm not blushing.'

'I should have remembered you don't like that sort of talk. They used to pull your leg about it in El Vino's, I remember. I'd have thought the navy would cure all that.'

'Do I sound awfully starchy? I've been told so.'

'Only by people who don't really know you,' said Tom in a different tone of voice. 'To me, just shy. Do pour yourself another scotch, old son, and relax. The night is young. The First Sea Lord won't do anything to you as long as you can walk more or less straight up the gang-plank. Or you can still use the spare bedroom and stay over, if you won't be actually court-martialled. Be my guest.'

'I really must go and leave you to it.'

Sandy stood up. His legs were not as steady as he had thought they would be. His face was still embarrassingly red. He walked out on to the shallow balcony where he found the air was, of course, as oppressive as it was in the living room. The lights of the financial institutions in Central had died but the neon signs advertising the many entertainments in Wanchai were visible in the slight haze. Otherwise it was quite dark. The tailors' shops, each with a frontage of no more than nine or ten feet, were already closing. The restaurants and souvenir shops were still very much open, striking his eye as silver lines reaching into the centre of Hong Kong Island. Cabs squealed their way along Kennedy Road eight floors below, giving even louder squeals as they turned into or from Queensway at the foot of Kennedy Road. The square white tower on the narrow base which had once been HMS *Tamar*, the combined headquarters of the British Army, the Royal Navy and the Royal Air Force, loomed over Victoria Harbour like a ghost; its thirty storeys had already been taken over by something or other mainland Chinese, as the mainland Chinese would take over practically everything else that at present flew the British flag.

Depressed, Sandy stepped back into the living room. There was still no sign of May Fong. 'Anyway, even if duty didn't call, it would embarrassing, being your guest for . . . well, I mean, something like that . . . Not that she isn't nice. She's very nice . . . ' He didn't want to admit that his reticence had more to do with inexperience than morality: he was ashamed that he had never gone all the way.

Tom Webster said: 'If that's all that's bothering you, forget it. May and I understand one another. Don't worry about a thing. As I'm your host, I'll even settle the financial side of it. All part of uncle Tom's hospitality to a young man far from home.'

'You're laughing at me. You really mean you wouldn't mind? Bit cool, aren't you?'

'I might mind with just anybody but not an old friend. You sound as if you're having second thoughts. Sensible man. Of course I'm cool. Why should I mind?'

'I just thought – '

'That was always your trouble in Fleet Street, I seem to remember. Thinking. Very dangerous pastime.'

Tom Webster got up, his glass empty but his legs quite steady. He playfully punched Sandy on the shoulder, which made Sandy hotter and more uncomfortable than ever. What about the others in the HMS *War Lion* wardroom? They might well think he was an awful wally for hesitating when offered a good thing on a plate. He began thinking about whether he was cut out for roughing it at sea and commanding men.

Since he had first clapped eyes on her less than an hour ago, he had never stopped thinking and wondering about May Fong, her angelic face, her neat raven hair, her surprisingly full thighs. Could he handle it? Was he really about to burst? He had never had a woman. He blamed the backlash against the permissivism of the 1960s and 1970s, even though in his view that backlash was quite right and proper.

He nearly tripped over the edge of the carpet when Tom Webster suddenly said: 'Ah! She's coming back. She'll feel slighted if you don't, you know. I saw the way she kept looking at you. I'm not just relying on what she said about you when you took a leak yourself. Look, I'll run this suggestion past you. I'll make it easy for you. I fancy a walk anyway – it will get some fresh air into my lungs, if there's any left in Hong Kong. I'll be back in one hour. Time enough for you?'

Afterwards it was as if the night were not quite so oppressively airless. May Fong had certainly made it easy. The hour was almost up when she and Sandy finally tore themselves from one another, both covered in perspiration, Sandy gasping and May Fong quietly moaning.

The cool air blew on his face on his way back to the ship, berthed near what had been HMS *Tamar*. Sandy started to think of her with Tom Webster, and of what they might be doing together. It made him feel surprisingly uncomfortable, resentful and – yes – spent and empty. He must try to forget it.

He had had one more stiff whisky before leaving Tom and May to it. He must now concentrate on getting back aboard the ship without making an ass of himself by tripping on the gang-plank or something of that kind, the sort of thing he had been known to do even when completely sober. He was tired and yet more wide awake than he had ever felt. He was walking a foot above the pavements rather than on them.

When he got back to *War Lion* he must get some sleep and then try to forget her.

This was to prove difficult.

# 2

Walking along the well-lit Queens Road back towards Central,
Sandy met few people. All of them were Chinese, and all of
them looked through him as if he were not there. Some spat on
the pavement with noisy enthusiasm. Tom had warned him
not to take this as an anti-British demonstration: it was just
that Hong Kong had been described as the spitting capital of
the world. Sandy felt that his tweed sports jacket, as well as the
loud cheering going on inside him, should have made him easy
to notice, even though he was carrying the jacket over
his arm. Hong Kong's climate hardly encouraged any form of
display of Harris tweed.

Sandy had no intention of confessing, to Tom or anyone else,
his overwhelming relief that he was no longer a virgin. The very
word made his skin crawl. The state itself had made him painfully self-conscious, especially when he had first entered the
navy. He had often had to listen, at naval college and on his
training ship, to his fellow officers-in-training recounting their
successful amorous exploits. He had almost always smiled
politely. He hadn't believed all of them; he wasn't quite as naive
as Tom obviously still thought him. But they rankled all the
same, especially when, well into his twenties, he suddenly began
to feel quite old.

He passed the narrow shop of Wah Sun, the tailor recom-
mended to him by the more experienced officers on *War Lion*,
and decided that tomorrow he would get himself measured
for a lightweight jacket. Sweat was still pouring out of him,
though the night was turning cooler.

Just before Queens Road ended in the criss-cross of streets

near the financial district stood Jean-Paul's Restaurant. It had its menu in English as well as Chinese, the coded message that Europeans were welcome. The folding doors to the street were drawn back, exposing a wide bar area full of tables occupied mostly by young Hong Kong Chinese with white shirts, sober silk neckties and Rolex or Cartier wristwatches. Behind them, screened by low drapes suspended on brass rods, was the restaurant section. Here more elaborate and expensive food was served to usually older Europeans and Chinese.

Sandy turned back and took a seat at the only vacant table in the bar area. 'Coffee, please. Black.'

'You want milk?'

'Black. No milk.' Sometimes he thought the Hong Kong Chinese, faced with next year's takeover by the mainland Chinese, deliberately affected not to understand the English language any more. Damn silly of them, as they had used it quite happily for years. The coffee might not do him a lot of good – he was intoxicated by his experience even more than by Tom Webster's whisky – but it was better than nothing. Tom had not offered him coffee after that final whisky, obviously eager to turn his attention to May Fong.

Sandy drummed his fingers and hummed to himself during the long wait for coffee. What did he feel about Tom? Difficult to say. He was certainly grateful to him, as he had often been grateful in the past. That now made him feel ashamed. To be handed a woman like May as a gift or indulgence by another man was confoundedly humiliating. Or was it, really? If he had felt that strongly about it, he should surely have stuck to his original decision not to become involved. Now he was involved. When he remembered her heavy breasts, her strong writhing thighs, her smooth legs clasped around him for the third and fourth time, wasn't his irritation with Tom hypo-critical? Even at school, they had said of him that if he were not especially clever, he was at least honest. Was he being honest with himself now?

What was it that Tom had said? 'That was always your trouble back in Fleet Street, I remember. Thinking.'

Sandy laughed out loud till the look on the faces of the young Hong Kong Chinese at the next table persuaded him to disguise it as a cough and to reassume an impassive expression. He sipped his newly-arrived coffee and affected to watch the male Chinese at another table playing Mah Jong, the clicking of the ivory pieces on the table like angry crickets, the young faces of the players concentrated, oblivious of all else, including the girls with them. Surely even they must guess he was thinking about May and even what he was thinking about May? If they did, they didn't show it. He might not have been there, just as after next year he probably wouldn't be there ever again. For the Royal Navy, the world was getting smaller. Unlike Tom, he couldn't be facetious about things like that.

'Another coffee, please. No milk. You understand? You can take this milk away. No milk.' He pushed the milk jug away from him to make the point clearer.

Oh well. None of this would have happened to him at home in Henley-on-Thames or, for that matter, even in Fleet Street. He might have gone on for several more years carrying his celibate burden, every passing year making the confession of it more unthinkable. Girls just assumed you had done it and it would be the devil of a job confessing you hadn't. Damn it, he wasn't a complete ass: there had been one or two girls who might have been unaccountably eager to help him in that respect. They had never been the right girls. Always too hard-eyed, too pushy. He seemed to attract that sort; or at least until May Fong. With her lost mother and her younger brother and a younger sister she mentioned briefly and then never again, she was altogether different.

18

Of course she was what she was. But she had to be judged by different rules, customs and standards of behaviour, not to mention economic conditions. In other words the rules of brute survival. He felt a great rush of tenderness for her. He hadn't carried it off too badly, he felt. If she had been only pretending to enjoy it, she had pretended very well. But perhaps she was good at pretending, knowing that Tom would give her something extra – what? Twenty pounds? Fifty pounds? More than that? Had she only pretended?

The coffee still hadn't completely steadied him, so he asked for yet another. If he were worldly like Tom, he could judge whether she had been pretending or not. But if he were worldly, he wouldn't be here now, he'd have still been working in his father's estate agency. He had in fact left it after six months, claiming that some of the things said about the houses they were selling were not completely honest. His father had been hurt and bewildered when he had taken that Fleet Street news agency job he had seen advertised in the *Daily Telegraph*.

Sandy himself had thought that journalism might be a way of doing some good in the world, crusading for the truth and so on. Oh dear! He had hated visiting women made widows by air crashes. He could never remember what questions to ask them – though Tom, as chief reporter and later confidant, had gone as far as to write him out whole lists of suitable questions.

Only Tom seemed to want to bother with him, though at the same time even he was always pulling his leg. 'You should have been called George – St George with the white horse fighting the dragon.' And, with the sack looming, it had been Tom who had gently advised him to try something else before he got the bullet. 'Something more . . . structured, old son. You're going to need a job that's straighter than straight. This trade, this old black art, could distort your life – and the money's not good, either. Which is why it's becoming a job for well-connected prats who don't need the money. It could totally foul up a well-meaning soul like you.' Tom should know: five weeks later, that never very conspicuous marriage of his had cracked, and almost at once Tom had started looking for ways out of Fleet Street; out of Britain altogether.

The Royal Navy had been Sandy's father's rather grudging suggestion. Some dim and distant relative, it seemed, had been in the navy. Sandy had signed up rather than argue and had been surprised at how quickly he felt he belonged. It was a good life on the whole if you didn't mind taking and giving orders, and if you played it straight.

The coffee had done its work sufficiently well for him to notice immediately that the naval rating who had just stumbled in and flopped into a chair near the pavement was Ferguson. Hell. Every ship, he had been warned, had at least one habitual hard case aboard: Able Seaman Ferguson was HMS *War Lion*'s. Ferguson was a tall stooping man ten years older than Sandy. He had ginger hair, a pitted face, a broken nose and thin lips always halfway to a sneer. If there was ever any trouble, Ferguson was somehow involved, either directly or tangentially. Sandy saw immediately that Ferguson was drunk; quiet surly drunk, but drunk. He had knocked over an ashtray while sitting himself down and had trouble getting a cigarette into his mouth and lighting it.

Sandy hastily put down on the table enough money to cover the coffees plus a handsome tip and equally quickly walked out, taking no notice whatever of Ferguson. He pointedly didn't see him. If there was going to be trouble, he didn't want to be involved. Not tonight, when he rather wanted to kiss the whole world.

Luck was not with him. As he got nearer to the ship, he heard stumbling footsteps behind him. Reluctantly he looked round. Of course it was Ferguson: obviously the waiters at Jean-Paul's had also noticed he was drunk and had promptly moved him on; perhaps his history of trouble extended to that establishment as well as *War Lion*. Sandy got the impression that Ferguson was deliberately walking behind him mimicking his own walk.

He ignored it, not even turning round to look again when he had to stop and prove his identity to the Royal Marine on the harbour gates. Inside the gates, Ferguson's flopping footsteps were still behind him. Sandy was within sight of the *War Lion*'s gang-plank when Simons suddenly overtook him on a bicycle, swaying from side to side.

Sandy swore under his breath. If Ferguson was the hard case of the ship, the small, plump and pasty-faced Simons was its soft case: the idiot, the bungler who could make almost as much trouble for himself and others by not trying as Ferguson could by trying. Over-staying his leave, forgetting to do his rostered cleaning jobs, spilling ketchup over his trousers or, on one memorable if inexplicable occasion, spilling it over his white-topped uniform cap.

Simons reached the gang-plank, jumped off the bike, hurled it into the water, and started swaying up the gang-plank.

The gang-plank should have been manned at all times. It was not manned now. There was no Regulator or delegated Able Seaman at the top of it; no one official, in other words, to be a witness to the disposal of an obviously stolen bicycle except himself and Ferguson behind him.

Sandy quickly turned to establish where Ferguson was. Ferguson was standing perfectly still behind him like an old fox, obviously wondering what this young officer would do or not do, and how he could create dissension from it.

'Simons!' shouted Sandy. 'Stay where you are. Ahoy! Is there anyone up there manning the gang-plank? Ahoy! Anyone?'

By the time the bemused Simons had got the message, stopped and turned around, another rating appeared at the double at the top of the gang-plank, where he should have been all the time.

'This gangway should be manned at all times,' said Sandy. He tried to keep his voice clipped and official. He was well aware that Ferguson's hard eyes were boring into the back of his neck, and that it would have been better if all this had occurred on some other evening. But at least he was now stone cold sober.

'I was up here all the time, sir.'

'You saw this man throw a certain article into the harbour, then? What was it? Tell me.'

The pause was a long one. 'Don't know, sir.'

'Then you weren't manning the gang-plank, were you? This man has just thrown a bicycle into the water. I hardly imagine it was his own. Take his name, report him to the duty Regulator or his deputy, and report yourself as well for failure to man the gang-plank. Is that clear? The Captain or his designated officer will sort all this out.'

'Sir, I was here all the time – '

'Not when Simons threw the bloody bicycle into the water you weren't, or you'd have seen what it was,' snapped Sandy. He remembered that an officer was supposed never to argue nor justify himself. Nevertheless he found himself saying, 'Trouble with the local population is just what we don't want at this moment. You've had that point spelled out to you often enough.'

'But, sir – '

'That's enough. One more word out of you, whatever your name is, and it'll be a very serious matter. You hear me?'

Too heavy-handed! His approach should have been different, but what should it have been, exactly? He didn't know. Things surely couldn't go as badly for him as if Ferguson had been able to leak it to the entire ship that he hadn't been tough enough. He cursed Ferguson silently. The object of his curses, he noticed, had now moved into his line of vision.

'May I pass, sir? Have I your permission to do that, sir, or do you require any assistance, sir?'

It was all said, especially the three sirs, with such mock helpful insolence that Sandy knew Ferguson was still sober enough to be real trouble if handled the wrong way.

'Go ahead, Ferguson, by all means. That is, unless you have a stolen bicycle about your person and are thinking of disposing of it into the harbour.'

Ferguson didn't even pretend to laugh politely. Sandy hadn't really expected him to: his own placatory joke had been as big a mistake as his original harshness with the man on the gangplank. He wished they would all go to hell and leave him to think about May Fong.

He pushed past Simons and went to his own quarters. The whole thing was too trivial for words and when the Captain or the second officer heard the case, it would all no doubt be ironed out and soon forgotten.

In this he was gravely mistaken.

# 3

'You did what you had to do about this prat Simons. Let him stew in his own juice and let the other trouble-maker say what he likes. You've got the rank, he hasn't. You're making no more sense about Simons than you are about May.'

'Not that again. I thought you liked her.'

'I do like her. She does what she does and she's very good at it. I should keep that in mind all the time. I do.'

Sandy Britton felt he couldn't tell Tom that he always had her in mind; had always had her in mind since their meeting. It was Saturday night. They were on the way up to Hong Kong's highest point, The Peak, by railcar, the so-called Peak Tram, which ran steeply up the side of the mountain. Sandy's stomach kept turning over; the effect was not really as if the railcar were climbing at a steep angle, but more as if the railcar were level while the tall apartment blocks on either side of the line leaned sickeningly backwards, as if about to topple over.

Sandy said at last: 'You don't really think of her as a human being at all, do you? That's the truth of it.'

'As you would say, what rot. I do think of her as a human being – with her living to earn. I let her get on with her work and her life and I ask no questions. That's not as insensitive as you may think. What makes you think she regards you and me as human beings? In her mind we may be no more than income. Some questions are best left unexplored.'

'You said she didn't charge extra, which she could have done.'

'That was odd, I grant you. When I told you she fancied you, I thought she did fancy you, but I didn't think she'd fancy anyone quite as much as that. Let's just say I'm a good client, so perhaps she thought of it as a loss leader or discount . . . Oh come on, Sandy, that was supposed to be funny. Where's your sense of humour?'

Sandy looked glumly out of the railcar window. The railcar was packed, as Tom had said it always was on Saturday nights. Prosperous Chinese, visiting Europeans, Japanese tourists and members of the British Forces were making their way to the restaurants and bars at The Peak. It overlooked the harbour and the shimmering Pacific beyond it, its more remote and ill-lit gravel pathways the hideout for lovers.

'You can be pretty cynical sometimes,' Sandy said at last.

'Just realistic.'

They were sitting at the rear of the railcar. In front of them stood gaping passengers, blocking much of the view. One or two younger Chinese stood directly facing them, craning their necks to watch, and giggle over, the steep shiny rails they were climbing. On the left of the railcar, periodically treading on Sandy's feet, was a middle-aged American tourist with a loud check jacket and a loud complaining wife in a long belted suede coat.

'Are you sure this thing is safe, Bobbie? Didn't I read some place it crashed?'

'That was some place else, Adelaide, and years back. They completely renovated this Peak Tram in the 1980s.'

Most of the other occupants of the railcar were young Hong Kong Chinese, with a sprinkling of Chinese mainland visitors, recognisable by their plainer clothes. Most were facing towards the front of the railcar, their backs to Sandy and Tom. One Chinese girl with neat black hair, standing directly in front of him, looked like May Fong until she suddenly turned round, when she revealed teeth with gaps and eyes set too close together: not like May Fong at all. The girl beside her could have been May, too, but her little scream when the railcar gave a judder was shrill, nothing at all like May's voice. What was May doing at this moment? That was too painful to think about, though that was just what he was doing; what he had been doing every moment since last night.

'Realistic? What's so unrealistic about thinking about her as a human being, hearing her out when she talks about herself and about trying to support her young brother?'

'I seem to remember she had an older brother. That was the version I got.'

'Older brother, younger brother, what's it matter? Her English isn't perfect. I believe her.'

They were nearing The Peak: Sandy could feel the air becoming thinner and chillier. The water of the harbour below them shimmered like a distorting mirror.

'I didn't say I didn't believe her,' said Tom Webster. 'I just pointed out that her story seems to change from time to time in certain details. I don't blame her, but – '

'Forget the details. What's the gist of it, as far as you know? Did she get here illegally from China in the first place?'

'I doubt that. At one time you used to be able to stay in Hong Kong once you'd been here a certain time, even if you'd got here illegally in the first place. But they altered that back in the eighties. Thousands of illegal immigrants had been pouring in across the border in the late seventies. Hundreds in one day. It had to be stopped.'

'Then how come a girl her age was allowed to come over the border legally? If she's been here four years, which she told me she had been, she must have been sixteen at most when she arrived. Just a kid.'

'Yes, well . . . The details do vary. I suspect they all came in with their father. May doesn't talk about him much. I'd guess he brought the children here in search of fame and fortune, and then simply disappeared when things didn't turn out as he hoped, leaving the children to fend for themselves. It happens. May's been mother and father to her brother and her younger sister – if she's got one. Or so I rather gather from what she's let on. But as I said, the details do seem to vary.'

'That would be so like her. But what a father! Fine specimen.'

'Difficult to judge. Lots of Chinese have got here somehow, thinking the streets are paved with gold, and have got their fingers burnt. They don't all come for ideological reasons, you know – it's usually money. A lot who came in the seventies, when the rush was at its peak, were crooks – the mainland Chinese were probably bloody glad to get shot of them. May's father sounds a bit like that to me. It would figure.'

'That makes me think more of her, not less. She must have had a hard life. A bloody hard life.'

'Not as hard as if she'd been ugly . . . All right, all right, sorry! Anyway, it seems the mother stayed behind in China – why isn't clear. I haven't pressed her on it. It doesn't seem as if May has heard from her, or of her, for years. She talked about it once. She began to cry. I gave her some extra dollars, quite a few. You're not quite the only fool in the world.'

'You think she's never sincere, don't you?'

'Difficult to say. It must be difficult for her to be what you call sincere, wouldn't you say? It could have been crocodile tears to soften up a client, I suppose; perhaps not. I don't know. Let and let live.'

'I'm sure it was genuine about her mother. Why shouldn't it be?'

Tom Webster pointed out some sights on the skyline. Then he said slowly, 'You're a good chap, Sandy. It can be dangerous, you know, trying to be too pure in a very impure world – especially out here. As I say, the details tend to change and change again. The Oriental mind, perhaps.'

'Oh, come on! I've known you to embroider anecdotes yourself, Tom, I'm not that stupid. Is there any difference? People do embroider. I don't think you're nearly as cynical as you pretend.'

'Then I must work harder at it. If I were an utter cynic, however, I'd say that there was a rather impolite description of the state of mind you appear to be in.'

'Tell me.'

'Cunt-struck. That's what they call it.'

The American couple overheard this. The woman in the long suede coat glared at them with disapproval, her horrified wrinkled white face suggesting that Tom had indecently exposed himself rather than merely used a four-letter word.

Tom didn't noticeably lower his voice. 'Cunt-struck,' he repeated.

Sandy kept his temper. 'Look, she didn't want to talk about herself at all in the first place. She only told me because I asked her questions about it. She said it didn't matter about her mother, but there she was just being brave, I think. I told her that of course it mattered, a lost mother was bound to matter, just as a younger brother who relied on her mattered. And if she was so anxious to spin pure unadulterated lies about herself, why did she keep dodging the issue of her younger sister, after she'd let it out by accident that she had one? You didn't even know she had one, did you?'

'Look, my star-crossed lover, I still don't know for certain she has one, and neither do you. Perhaps her younger brother changes his sex to suit the circumstances and the client, how do I know? You only know what she told you. It's far better, believe me, to listen politely and not to question her or any other bar girl too closely. That's the etiquette in that sort of situation; that's the protocol. As a naval man, you should have a feeling for protocol and all that sort of thing.'

'She was quite open about her mother. She doesn't know where she is.'

'Maybe the woman has gone to earth, maybe the woman doesn't know about her daughter, doesn't care. Perhaps her older or younger brother, or her younger sister, whatever version you prefer, is pushing heroin – it's a growth industry over here since the British grip began to slacken, at least that's what some of my contacts say.'

'Tom, is your news agency a cover for MI6 or the CIA? That's also what some people say.'

Tom Webster looked at him sharply. Then he laughed. The laugh wasn't quite convincing. 'Just an honest job of journalism, old chum – one that took me out of bloody Britain, which is a bloody good place to be out of these days . . . Ah! We're here.'

'That chap you share a desk with. The one that came down with us in the lift when I called for you . . . '

'Oh, he's CIA all right, at least people say he is, but that's his freelance activity, so to speak. Everybody knows about it; perhaps it improves the image of an otherwise rather dull man. Did you notice his hairpiece? Proclaims itself like an eighteenth century town crier. The poor man can't keep anything secret, even his hair.'

'I'm glad I'm just a simple sailor.'

'Spoken like an officer and a gentleman. Now do be careful not to get yourself trampled in the crush when the doors open. There's always a stampede.'

'I can take care of myself.'

Sandy managed to say it with a laugh. It was his last laugh for some time. As he walked into the restaurant, his tweed jacket over his arm – he hadn't been able to collect his new lightweight jacket from Wah Sun – he spotted her immediately as if some instinct had turned his eyes into the far left corner, under the potted palms. This time it really was May Fong. His heart began to thump and his mouth suddenly went very dry.

She was wearing very little make up, except for silver lines under her eyes, which matched the silver lame dress which hugged her body and made it look like that of a precocious sixteen year-old dressing up beyond her years. A red scarf was tied loosely around her slender neck. In the soft lighting her skin was more like pure ivory than ever. She really was as beautiful as he remembered. She was sitting at a round corner table with a portly, far from young Chinese man with a shaven skull. He was wearing a finely-cut blue three-piece pin-striped suit, the waistcoat displaying a gold watch chain. Sandy found the sight nauseating.

Tom Webster saw her at almost the same moment as Sandy. 'Where are you off to, now, old son?'

'I'm getting out of here. It's embarrassing.'

'Not before we've eaten, you're not! I only had a sandwich at midday and I don't intend to go on hunger-strike just because she's here with another fella. Have some sense.'

'All right, since you're so eager to keep me here, we'll go over and say hello.'

'We'll do nothing of the sort, idiot. Protcol! There's an etiquette to cover this sort of situation. They manage these things in a very genteel way over here – this isn't Soho, you know. The etiquette's simply not to see her, right? She isn't there. Not even the merest nod on the way out, if she's still there – which judging from the eager gleam in her wealthy friend's eye, she probably won't be.'

Sandy said quickly: 'You can't blame her. Not many Europeans like us will still be around next year. She's got to think of her own future, if nobody else will.'

'Quite so. Well said. Highly noble. But do I detect a certain edge of disillusionment in your voice?'

Sandy flopped into a chair at the table to where they had been directed by the head waiter, relieved that it was nowhere near May's table, though he still had her in full if distant view.

'Okay, Sandy, I'll change places with you if you don't want to see her.'

'I'll stay where I am, thank you.'

'As you please.'

Sandy wanted not to look at her, but his eyes periodically disobeyed his mind. Tom talked on and on about the other places in Hong Kong he must be sure to visit.

'Penny for your thoughts, chum,' said Tom, evidently noting at last that he had lost his audience. 'On second thoughts, don't bother. I can guess your thoughts. Look, old son, how long's your ship here for? A week? Ten days? Then you sail away. It's no good, you know, really it isn't.'

'You think I'm pretty ridiculous, one way and another, don't you?'

Tom Webster's voice softened. 'Did I say so? I did not. When I think so, I'll probably tell you. At the moment I just think you're rather young. Yes, chum, you're just suffering from that dangerous medical condition called youth, from which you may recover in time, though thousands don't. I recommend having the squid and giving the house wine a miss. What about some claret? We can be pretty sophisticated out here, you know. All the best French plonk. What the new bosses will say to that, I don't know, so drink up while you can.'

Sandy detected what he thought of as Tom's lecturer's tone. He looked again at May Fong. 'Anything that will make me plastered quick will do.'

He turned his head back to watch Tom Webster's loud theatrical sigh. Blast the man, he was old, old. Just to make it clear he wasn't going to be pushed around, Sandy insisted on Beaujolais rather than claret in his most firm naval officer's voice, and emptied the glass almost immediately after the attentive waiter filled it.

# 4

Mr Hok thrust into her like an old bull determined to prove its strength. He was May Fong's most enthusiastic client, and the richest. He was also the most discreet: none of his organisations bore his name. If he succeeded in taking her five times, he was generous with extra banknotes, and she well knew by now how to help him achieve this aim without appearing to help him at all. She was never too sure about his age: she supposed it could have been anything from forty to sixty. As a vain stud, he could have been thirty or less.

Mr Hok – he was rarely referred to as anything else by those who had business with him – gritted his teeth. His pugnacious face was covered in sweat. His head was suspended above hers as he supported himself on the palms of his hands, arms extended, for the fifth try. He was gasping, exposing his yellow teeth. His hands were on either side of her head. He was watching her face intently, so that she had to half close her eyes and pretend to be carried away . . . to disguise her wish that it was somebody else, someone with young fair hair rather than a bristle of old grey hair, someone who would almost melt into her, not push himself into her in this crude way which hardly took account of her or what she might be feeling.

For a few seconds she became panicky. It seemed as if he would not manage it the fifth time. If he failed, he tended to notice things he would not otherwise notice. She tightened herself around him, gave a realistic gasp and told herself she could make him come, whatever she was thinking or not thinking. He was not the sort of client with whom you dare risk sneaking a look at the wall clock, let alone your wristwatch.

The sun through the picture windows of the bedroom at the back of Mr Hok's magnificent east-facing house. He usually preferred it in the daylight, even if this time he had not wanted to wait until daylight until he entered her for the first time. A fifth time on this sunny Sunday morning would leave him obviously satisfied and expansive, the mood in which he most often offered her presents. The rays of the sun now reflected into the bedroom from the blue surface of the swimming pool outside. The pool was encircled on three sides by the white house, which was one of the grandest in Kowloon, that part of the Hong Kong colony that stood on the mainland between Hong Kong island and the less developed New Territories. The house was worthy of one of the richest men in Hong Kong, a man with no wife or known dependants, a man moreover with a reputation for honesty in his dealings – at least as far as any rich man, with his fingers in so many profitable pies, could be regarded by the envious as honest.

May Fong gave him another realistic little sigh, remembering that she had much to be grateful for as far as Mr Hok was concerned. Just being in the house made her feel good. The knowledge that she could still interest him after several months made her feel even better. She never know exactly why Oriental men, except for that diminishing band of Hong Kong Chinese who wished to imitate European men in everything, should be interested in her, though objectively she knew they could be: her face was too white, too long and too different from that full-cheeked roundness which Orientals usually regarded as beauty; her teeth were too white. In this respect she was lucky to have found the appreciative Mr Hok. He did seem to have had European tastes for some little while. For instance the bedroom was light and airy, with curtains of western geometric pattern, the Chinese lantern hanging from the centre of the plain white ceiling being the only sign that it might be the home of a Chinese.

Mr Hok came for the fifth time.

The lantern swung gently in the breeze above their heads. Perhaps Mr Hok made a point of noticing nothing that would entail loss of face if seen, including sometimes her true feelings. Of course it had been stupid of her, when leaving the restaurant, to walk the few extra paces to the table where Sandy sat with Tom Webster, and to greet both men. That could have offended her regular client Tom Webster as well as her regular client Mr Hok. She had simply been drawn to the table, as if her legs were on a different wavelength to her head. That fact made her angry. Sandy had looked surprised, open-mouthed with surprise, running a hand over his golden head. Tom Webster had looked even more surprised – he knew, and must know she knew, that it was a breach of all the rules on which her business was based. She just could not have avoided walking to the table at which Sandy sat.

For some seconds, such memories of the previous evening got in the way of what Mr Hok was now saying to her. She didn't notice, either, that his hand was extended with more than the usual number of Hong Kong banknotes. Always after the fifth time he paid her not only her fee for the whole night but also about half that again for her own pocket; this time her personal sum was almost equal.

'I am so sorry, I did not hear you,' she said. It was part of her job to have good manners, never to let her own feelings show – certainly never her feelings of detachment or boredom.

'I said I will double this,' he said in his slow, rasping voice which still had traces of a Cantonese accent, this time lying back on the huge bed and watching her instead of climbing into his clothes straight away as he normally did. 'Call it part of your future allowance. This is my proposition. You move in here, you get rid of other entanglements with my help, you stay here for five years guaranteed.'

For several seconds what she was being asked did not sink in. Then she did not know what to say. She saw now that for the whole of this visit he had been leading up to something but she had been unable to guess what. The proposition nearly took her breath away. She swung her legs over the side of the bed, her back towards him, so that he could not see her face. Now she understood well enough. Perhaps the idea had been close to surfacing several times before, but had never quite happened until her arrival at Sandy's table in the restaurant had sent out danger signals. It was altogether odd the idea was surfacing now, just at the point when she might be unable to force herself to accept it.

'You mean you want me to stay here with you – permanently? To live here?'

'Five years guaranteed.'

'Your wife would not object?'

'No wife. I tell you that before. No wife! I have a very nice house here, big staff but no wife.' His harsh voice suggested that he had known times rather different from his present wealth. How strange it was that she knew so little about him, except what was provided by the local press and by rumour, both of which she mistrusted.

'You have a very nice house, yes, certainly.' There was a great distance between herself and what was happening to her. Except for one thing. A week ago she might have jumped at it, seen it as the opportunity of a lifetime. As this man's mistress she would have security and a measure of respect for five years and perhaps more if she kept alert; as Mr Hok looked after her she could, in her turn, look after those who depended on her. Many such women had contrived to marry their protectors, and had ended up even more rich and secure. It was not to be despised, with the Chinese takeover of Hong Kong, and its uncertain affects on people like her, only a matter of months away. Last week she would have been confident that she could have continued to please Mr Hok quite easily; now she only wanted to please one man; and the only way she could continue to see that man was to evade this offer and continue at least for a while in her present way of life.

'It is such a surprise,' she said, wishing to keep his respect, not to offend him. She wrapped the bed covers around herself.

Mr Hok pulled them aside and took a long hard look at her. 'You are perhaps worried about . . . your existing commercial loyalties?' He gave a thin smile.

She assumed he was talking about those people behind her employment. These were people one did not talk about, ever. They might or might not have connections with the Triad gangs – it was better not to wonder, let alone ask.

In the circumstances it was better for her to say nothing. Mr Hok continued to smile. He moved away from her, still smiling, his eyes still on her. He did up the zip of his elegantly pressed cavalry twill trousers, slipped on a striped silk shirt from the huge fitted wardrobe, and slipped the shirt into his trousers. What an air of assurance and power he radiated, without doing or saying anything very much. The certainty that his money could move mountains; could save him from any enemies. Or perhaps he too was also worried about next year and what Chinese rule might bring; perhaps he was seeking some sort of comfort and security of his own? You had to watch for men's vulnerabilities as well as their strengths.

'I am a man of means. I would of course take care of the financial side of releasing you from your present . . . obligations. I am in a position to do so. You need fear trouble from nobody. They are reasonable men. All men are reasonable when the money is right.'

She was now trembling. She wanted to get away and think. She wished she could get into her clothes without seeming in a hurry to leave. Her clothes were on the chair where he had thrown them only a few hours ago. Just to talk about those sort of men made her feel frightened and sick: usually it was only the Europeans, and the stupidest gweilos at that, who joked about people like the Triads. She looked away from him again so that he could not see her eyes.

'Next year,' he said, 'the Europeans will no longer be in control. A lot of big men will be smaller men but I will still be big. It will be the time for having the right sort of friends. Good friends. I can be a very, very good friend.'

No doubt he meant well, but his persistent words badgered her. She still said nothing. She could think of nothing to say.

'Think of your family,' he said. 'Your mother – I have contacts, I think I could help you find her. We must take care of her, of course. Think of your brother. I have friends in the police. Think of your young sister.'

She looked at him sharply. 'I have no younger sister!'

'I understood – '

'I may have said that to you before I knew you well. I confess it – it was to win your sympathy. Yes. I am sorry about that wicked trick.'

'It is the way of the world to tell lies, especially if they are lucrative lies. We will agree that you have no younger sister.'

His indulgent tone jarred on her. 'I tell you I have no younger sister!'

'Of course not, as you say. Will you think over what I have said? Will you consider my offer carefully?' He might have been a company chairman offering to take over a rival business. She thought of Sandy's white face, his large blue eyes and his fair hair. 'Five years guaranteed,' he persisted. 'Where would you get a better offer?'

'I have no sister. You do not believe me. You are making me angry, I think.' The anger was half real, half a way of evading for a bit more time having to respond in any way to his proposition.

He stood there smiling down at her. There was a long uncomfortable silence. 'I will wait,' he said at last. 'I am a patient man. Much may be gained by waiting.'

She did not give him an answer. She got up from the bed, briskly ignoring her nudity, and dressed quickly. It was not until she was back in the silver lame dress and had brushed and pulled her hair back into tight smoothness that she felt safe – or as safe as she could feel when two men were busy disrupting her life, one by openly trying to talk about buying her from Them and also disbelieving her about a younger sister, the other by making her uncertain about what she might do next.

'I think about it,' she said at the bedroom door. She did not know what other answer to give, however certain the answer might have been if the old bull had made her the proposition a week ago.

# 5

It was a ritual quite strange to Sandy. He felt an awful ass. Especially as, for all he knew, some of the respectably dressed men already at the long bar of the Hot Cat Club could be naval men in civilian clothes who might recognise him.

The lights of the long narrow bar, after the Wanchai district's garish streets full of neon advertisements, were too dim for him to recognise anybody, though those inside might well be able to recognise him. He stood just inside the door, blinking. The bar was only a third full. Sunday night might be a slack night. It might even be her evening off, if she had one. The thought made his heart sink. But at least if she were here somewhere, he would have a better chance of having her to himself.

The walls were a dark red, so dark they appeared almost black in the low light of the bulbs inside the gilt Chinese lanterns, from which red cut-outs of cats were suspended. Sandy could just about see that the woman who approached him was unusually fat for a Chinese, and heavily made-up. She could be between thirty and sixty: the grey puddingy features revealed little except that life had probably not been easy. She wore a flowing red dress with half-sleeves that revealed fat dimpled arms.

Sandy didn't know what one said in such circumstances. To his relief, she spoke first.

'I am Madam Cat. You want a drink, my dear? You go to my bar, you will be served. You are fine respectable man. Make yourself comfortable.'

Comfortable. It was not the first word that sprang to mind to describe his state of mind. Should he say straight away that a drink wasn't what he wanted, he wanted to see May Fong? Better not. Play it by ear.

'Oh!' he heard himself saying in what seemed to be a high pitched, embarrassed screech. 'Yes. Right.'

Seated at the long ill-lit bar facing a range of drinks bottles against a large mirror, most of them bottles with gold tops as if they might be champagne, he felt more conspicuous than ever. A couple of men seated side by side who he had passed on the way in looked round at him, then swivelled their eyes to the front again rather like robots. Behind the bar, a young Chinese girl in a sheer silk top which revealed much cleavage, frilled red panties and red fishnet stockings over shapely thighs, was already reaching for one of the bottles.

The silence, after the buzzing street sounds of Wanchai, was eerie. The sound of his own voice, as he said, 'Whisky, please,' boomed out unnaturally; in the streets it might not have been heard. The buses screeching round corners, the cabs hooting at other cabs, the heavy lorries, the shouts of some stall holders who even at this hour were still trying to sell bales of cloth, Hong Kong-made cheap polyester shirts, live fish, spectacle frames, CDs and vegetables, went unheard inside Madam Cat's dim domain.

Two of the girls stood at the furthest end of the bar, talking to two men in discreet whispers. As Sandy slid on to a high red bar stool, they all left together. The ruddy-faced man in the light grey suit, who could have been one of the crew of the Canadian Navy ship in the harbour or could have been British, threw what seemed a large amount of notes and coins on to the bar.

Sandy's order of whisky was ignored. The girl behind the bar said: 'No whisky. You have this.' She handed him a glass of what tasted like sweet Chinese wine diluted with sparkling mineral water, and a bill for an amount in dollars that startled him.

He was tempted to push the drink away and insist that if he were going to be robbed, he would at least be robbed drinking the drink he wanted. He changed his mind. He wanted no trouble. The essential issue was, where was May? Was she somewhere here? Had she left with a client? He should have phoned first, but there was no Hot Cat Club in the telephone directory. He was feeling more and more bloody foolish by the minute, but was determined to see her on his own initiative, without having to accept Tom or anyone else's assistance.

'You are looking for young lady?'

Madam Cat, or whatever her real name was, had taken a stool beside him at the bar. He correctly interpreted this as an invitation, or more likely command, to offer her a drink at, no doubt, her own hellishly inflated prices. She accepted what looked like the same Chinese sweet white wine diluted with sparkling mineral water, for which he paid a similar amount. He wanted to throw the drink at her; all this had absolutely nothing to do with the May he knew, or the way he was feeling. But if he walked out, how would he find her?

'You not hear me? You are looking for young lady?'

'Yes, as a matter of fact, I am.' He was sure he sounded like a curate announcing a hymn number. He felt his face going red.

'The one at the end of the bar who has just taken her seat, you see? She is a very good girl, clean of course, obedient or dominant, knows how to please a gentleman.'

'Actually I was looking for one girl in particular. May. May Fong.' Too eager.

'You know her?'

'We met at the home of a mutual acquaintance.' The hymn-announcing curate was back again. Others in the bar could overhear. He wished he could have collected his new light-weight jacket today rather than tomorrow.

'So! She is not here.'

'So I see. Is Sunday her evening off?'

Madam Cat laughed. 'She should be back,' she said with a quick look at a diamond and redstone encrusted wristwatch, 'in one hour.'

He knew what this meant. She was with a client. He was more hot and flustered then ever. But what had he expected? To be told she'd gone to church? 'One hour. I see.'

'You like to wait? You get me another drink?'

'I think I'll go now and come back later.'

'She may have found another friend before you return. You wait, yes?'

'All right.'

He ordered another drink for both of them, expecting that the price might have gone down, the original staggering price being merely an admission charge, as it were. The price hadn't gone down. He decided, since the only other available drink on show seemed to be real champagne – at least if the labels hadn't been tampered with – to stick to the white wine and sparkling mineral water muck. One drink later, he decided that rather than drink any more of it, he would have the cheapest real champagne available after all. Just as well he had only recently drawn his pay and, at sea, had little to spend it on. He was halfway though the bottle, with some mercifully spasmodic assistance from Madam Cat, when May Fong walked through the door alone.

His heart jumped as if someone had punched him there. She was wearing a tight black sheath of a dress, and white very high-heeled shoes. Her black hair, done up very high on her head like when he had first seen her, gleamed even in the poor light.

She walked over to him at once. 'San-di! You are here. Why are you here?'

He slid off the bar stool and looked down at the curves of

her body. 'Looking for you, as a matter of fact. Join me in a drink.'

'I check first with Madam Cat, please.'

'I checked first with Madam Cat. She knows all about it. She told me when you'd be back.'

She laughed, looking even younger. 'I very glad I am back quick for you, San-di.'

'Shall I pour you a glass?'

'I pour you one, San-di!' She slid on to a bar stool beside his own. The remaining men in the bar turned sideways to look at them. Let them look. For the first time that night, he felt in charge of things, as if he hadn't made such a hash of it, after all, as if he could look them or anybody else in the face. She was with him, laughing in that soft, delicate voice.

'I wanted to see you,' he said. 'Badly.'

'Yes? Is nice to see you, San-di.' The professional voice, or did she mean it? After all, she had walked over to talk to him in that restaurant at The Peak, and there was no reason why she should have done that unless she had really wanted to: Tom had been boring afterwards about how it wasn't the done thing.

'I wanted to spend some time with you, May.'

'You want me to go with you to the flat of your friend?'

'Not exactly, no.' He didn't at all like the prospect of that idea. To ring Tom up and ask him if he could take May there would be . . . well, bloody demeaning. Of course Tom would agree, pass it off with one of his cynical remarks, but he didn't want to rely on Tom's permission. And he had to think practically, too. How could he possibly enjoy being with her if this time Tom decided he wouldn't conveniently go out for an hour or so? If he stayed in the living room, where sounds from the bedroom could easily reach him?

'How you mean, not exactly, San-di? Please?'

'Well, I thought perhaps your place – '

44

She shook her head decisively. 'No, is not suitable. You take me to the flat of your friend.'

'No.'

'Why no?'

'I don't know. I just assumed that your apartment. . . . '

'That I would have a big apartment, like your friend's?'

'I wouldn't say it's all that big . . . '

'I would. Yes, I would say so. Is very good apartment.'

'Look, May, I wish I had an apartment of my own, but I haven't. Certainly not in Hong Kong. I don't want to trouble Tom, and I can hardly take you back to the ship, I'm afraid.'

'No, that would put the . . . fat into the fire, San-di.'

The easy way she used his first name, but distorting the sound of it as if it were two very separate and lyrical words, made his heart leap. Part of him would be content just to sit here in the bar with her and talk; but Madam Cat might not be so content – certainly not if he didn't buy another bottle of something or other at a ludicrous price.

'Let me think,' he said. 'You think, too, perhaps we'll hit on something.' It was like being with his first girl friend, when he was still living at his parents' home, and trying to think of a place where they could be alone together; he had come half way round the world to Hong Kong, and still he had no place to go.

Meanwhile, they talked. She told him some more about her mother. When she had last heard of her, her mother had been in a commune near Canton which was concerned with fruit farming. May Fong said she had not a had a letter or any other form of communication from her for years. She spoke about her brother, who appeared to alternate between the mainland and Hong Kong, sampling the police cells of both, as one money-making scheme after another went wrong.

If Sandy soon forgot how time was slipping by Madam Cat

did not. She approached them, holding by the elbow an over-weight man Sandy recognised as an officer from HMS *War Lion*. He affected not to recognise him and the other man affected not to recognise him. Excellent! He was getting better and better at this sort of thing.

Madam Cat said: 'Here is a gentleman who wishes to see you privately. May.'

Madam Cat's voice had an edge to it. There was only one thing to do. Sandy produced his wallet and handed over some notes, more than enough to cover the overpriced drinks, to Madam Cat. Then he took May Fong's arm and helped her off the bar stool.

Once outside, they continued to walk the streets. May trotting in her high heels to keep up with him. When she wrung her ankle stepping on to a pavement, Sandy called a cab so that they could go on talking in it. He returned her to the club within the hour, silently cursing but seeing no way out, pushing more than enough dollars into her hand and turning away with reluctance as she walked back into the club.

Next evening he was back in the bar. This time, after a great deal of soul-searching, he had decided after all to bury his pride and make a preliminary telephone call to Tom. Okay, so it was humiliating in a way. But compromised time with May was better than pompously proud time spent walking the streets or sitting in the back of taxis.

# 6

He did not notice the scratch near her eye until he had taken her for the third time and was beginning to feel the far from unpleasant tiredness he had encountered before. He drew his fingers gently down her cheek.

'May, you've hurt yourself.'

'Is nothing.'

'It's quite a scratch. Not wide but deep. Shall I go and find something to put on it?'

'San-di, you are very sweet. We do not disturb Tom, since he say as soon as we get here he is tired and will go to bed. We make no noise. Is nothing, really.'

'How did it happen? Did you fall?'

'Yes, I fall. San-di, lie on your back, and I show you something you like.'

'Dear May. In a minute. I'm talking about that eye.'

'Eye will heal up itself, no problem.'

'May, I don't believe you did fall. If you fell you'd have bruised yourself, this is a deep thin cut.'

She had been leaning over him face forwards, her legs enclosing his thighs. She dropped over on to her side beside him, and lay on her back, staring at the ceiling. 'You like me best like this, San-di?'

He propped himself up on one elbow and looked down at her. Her face shone with perspiration, her nipples were erect in a way which would surely be difficult to fake – it was the way other officers on *War Lion* had said you could tell whether a woman was faking or not. 'May, I like you any way at all, you must know that by now. I think someone attacked you. Were

47

they after your handbag or something?' He stroked the cut again with his finger.

'San-di, tell me about yourself. You went to university? I wanted much to go to a university.'

'Naval college. Damnit, May, don't change the subject. Were you mugged or what?'

She turned her head away from him and talked to the pile of books piled up against the wall. 'San-di, no one would mug me.'

'What's that supposed to mean? Anyone can get mugged, certainly in London and I suspect in Hong Kong, too, according to . . . ' He was about to mention Tom's name, but didn't. Instead he said, running his finger down the cut again, 'Well? What's the truth?'

She shut her eyes. 'The truth. You must have the truth. Very well, San-di. Another girl at the club did it. Now you know the truth. Are you happy?'

'How could I be happy when you're hurt? Was she drunk or something?'

'Jealous.'

'Of what?'

'All right, San-di. Last night when you came to the club, remember? A big girl in the corner with a red dress that hardly cover anything. She was still there when I came back to the club. You must have seen her.'

'I was waiting for you to come back. I didn't notice much else, I'm afraid.'

'She had been trying to make you notice her, till all the other girls, they laugh. Oh, San-di, all the other girls, they notice it. Once she come to you and ask for a light for her cigarette and you tell her you do not smoke and you look back towards the door. You do not notice things, San-di.'

'I didn't this girl, that's a fact.'

48

'When I get back to the club, she is still there. She tell me my mother was a – I do not like to say the words.'

'I see. All because of me, and I didn't know anything about it. I'm sorry, May, I'm really sorry.'

He leaned down to kiss her lips but she bent her head forward and he kissed her forehead instead. A great wave of tenderness welled up within him. 'Strange I know hardly anything about you, and yet . . . How long have you been in Hong Kong, May?'

'We come here with my father three, four years ago. Tell me about your father and mother.'

'Well, my father's an estate agent and I used to work for him before I went into the navy.'

'You could not get on with your father?'

'Oh, he was all right really. It was my mother who didn't think much of me.'

She sat up and looked down at him. She held his cheeks between her hand and lowered her face and kissed him. Several minutes later she said: 'Was she cruel to you, San-di?'

His tongue was sore where she had drawn it hungrily into her mouth. At first he spoke with difficulty. 'No, no, not cruel, just didn't see much in me, I suppose. She despised my father's job, I suppose, and wanted something better for me. She'd have liked me to be terribly bright and gone off to Oxford and got a double first and all that sort of thing. That wasn't me. I just don't have it on top.'

'On top, please?'

'Brains. I don't have those sort of brains. Don't have much, I suspect, in her eyes. Maybe she's right.'

'No, San-di, you have much. You are honest, I think. You are fine man.'

'Pity you can't tell her that.'

'Poor San-di. Poor San-di! I make you feel better.'

She did with great energy that Sandy was pretty sure was not put on.

Afterwards she said, 'I would have liked university, San-di. When my father bring my brother and sister here with me, I hope we all go to university, but my brother . . . poor boy, he get into trouble. He keep getting into trouble, my father cannot make much money because he breaks a leg and is handicapped, so I have to give him money as well as my brother.'

'You know something? It's the first time you've talked about your sister. You haven't done that before.'

She eased herself down on top of him and sought out his tongue again. He was only slowly conscious that she was looking at her wrist watch, the only item of apparel she had not removed.

'San-di,' she said in tones of great reluctance. 'I must get back to club or there is more trouble.'

'I'll walk you back there.'

'No.'

'Or we'll get a cab.'

'No, San-di.'

'Yes. You might get mugged.'

She lay a finger across his lips. 'I shall not be mugged, that will not happen. You rest here, San-di. Please. I find my own way out. I go back on my own.'

He swung his legs over the side of the bed and stood up so that he could feel in charge of things, but his nudity only made him feel foolish. His further protests, as she put on her clothes, were brushed aside.

'Look after that cut,' he said as she picked up her handbag. 'Please. I do feel responsible, you know.'

'San-di, you are funny but you are good man.' She kissed him lingeringly. She closed the bedroom door so quietly behind her so that he hardly heard it. He did not hear the front door of the apartment open or close at all.

# 7

Already Sandy wished he had gone straight back to the ship after May Fong had left shortly before midnight. Knocking on Tom's bedroom door had been a big mistake. Tom wouldn't miss the chance of making a big bit of psychodrama out of something like that.

'Okay, Sandy, I think we'd better talk,' he said, rolling out of bed and revealing assorted areas of dark matted body hair: even short-sleeved pyjamas were uncomfortable in this humidity. He climbed into a red towelling robe which had been slung over the back of a bedside chair, pushed thinning hair off his damp forehead, and then pushed Sandy back into the living room, where he stretched himself out on a bamboo framed sofa and helped himself from a rumpled packet of cigarettes on an occasional table.

'You don't, do you?' he enquired. 'Sensible man. Too bad you're not as sensible on all fronts.'

Sandy wished he had taken the time to put on more than his underpants. 'Oh? How do you mean?'

'I mean, old mate, that you may have got the script badly wrong.'

'I don't understand, Tom. Look, I'm sorry if us being here spoiled anything tonight.'

'Didn't spoil anything. I didn't touch her tonight, if that's what you want to hear. Not in the mood. I still think you've got the script all wrong.'

Sandy wanted to get back to the ship and think about May Fong. How could her beautiful dark eyes look so candid one second and so opaque the next? How could she lay in his arms like a lamb one second and become like a tiger the next? He said: 'I only knocked on your door to say thank you.'

'Bullshit. You knocked on the door to find out if May, after her tryst with you, was in my room with me. I don't need to be Sigmund Freud to work that out. I can only wonder at your state of mind, I can only assume you've not only got the script wrong but you've got the plot completely reversed.'

Sandy stopped pacing round the room and sat down on a cane chair, which creaked noisily. 'All right, Tom, I'll buy it. Am I being thick? What's all this about scripts and plots? What script and what plot?'

'Let it go. Maybe you'll be okay.'

'Don't worry about me.'

'Oh, I do worry about you. Who introduced you to the girl in the first place? She's pretty fussy about her clientele, you know. If it hadn't been for an introduction and a sound reference from me, as it were, you might not have got near her in the first place.'

'Really? What about those men I saw waiting in the Hot Cat Club?'

'Been doing your own research, I see. Good for you. They go on waiting unless Madam Cat likes the look of you. If you want to buy out any of Madam Cat's girls for a couple of hours, let alone a night, you need some sort of introduction, or there will be unexpected difficulties. The last thing Madam Cat wants at this time is trouble. Things like this are still run in a comparatively civilised way here: if you don't look the sort who's prepared to use a condom at all times, and that sort of thing, you won't get further than two glasses of Madam Cat's phoney champagne. It's not Soho low-life. That's why I'm not worried about your physical health, old chum, only your mental health.'

'I see. I'm bonkers now, is that it?'

'Like Hamlet, only mad Nor-Nor-West. Look, she's a bar girl. She is what she is. Her life is here. All right, she likes you, that's obvious. You like her. Fine. Your boat's in for – '

'Ship. Ship! It's called a bloody ship. A boat's something you row up the river.'

'Ship. I stand corrected. I stick to my point: your ship's in for what – ten more days? In a fortnight's time you'll be in another quarter of the globe entirely. You do see what I'm driving at?'

'Don't take me for an utter ass. I've seen your mind working from the start. You don't like your own routine interrupted, do you? Certainly not by any real feelings, your own or anyone else's.'

'Dear Sandy, I sometimes think that one day you may succeed in making me quite, quite angry. Not yet, perhaps, but I do see it as a vague future possibility. Feelings are something only within the scope of the under-twenty-fives? Is that what you think? Look, I like the girl myself. I'm fond of the girl. I have been for some time. The difference is, I know the script. I always give her some extra dollars for that dodgy brother – who, let me remind you, may not even exist. I listen to her. I don't say much, but I listen. But I don't get involved, I don't ask too many questions, especially those that might persuade her to give lies for answers. That's all I can do, I think. Don't look at me like that. Oh, I'm sorry for the casualties as British imperial control here nears its end, and all that sort of thing, but I can't simply wipe out the legacy of a hundred and fifty years of history and neither can you.'

'I don't try to wipe out history. Bugger history. Can't you sense she simply doesn't belong to . . . well, anything in the sort of life she's living? Can't you see she's special? Damn it, you talk enough about perception. Maybe you aren't being so bloody perceptive here.'

Tom Webster got up abruptly. 'It's too damp to argue. You know what you are? Not a frustrated idealist, a frustrated opera singer.'

'Opera now. What's that supposed to mean? All I know for certain sometimes is that the moment you see me, you take the piss. You did it in Fleet Street, and now you're doing it here. I don't like it much. If I'm so thick, I can't see why you bother with me at all. If you've got something to say, say it.'

'Right. I'd say you were reversing the role in the particular opera you're singing now. Wake up, Sandy. Madam Butterfly.'

'Madam Butterfly? Madam Butterfly? What's that got to do with anything? May can't make sense of you sometimes. You know what May said tonight? She said tonight, and I quote, that you were a "kind man who speaks strange things". Oh, I see I've embarrassed you at last. Someone thinking you kind?'

'Shall we stick to the point? Madam Butterfly, old son, the opera by Puccini. Quite a good opera for an Italian. The story of a misguided and dangerous infatuation. The gheisha who carries a torch for the American naval officer Pinkerton, who she expects to return to her when he sails away but who of course never returns. She came to a sticky end. You want that script for yourself, only with you doing the helpless, hopeless pining?'

'I don't go along with the word infatuation.'

'Not even when you knock on my bedroom door to check up on her, with your feeble excuse all ready?'

To his intense irritation, Sandy felt his face colouring up. Of course he had been checking up on her, but it was humiliating that it was so obvious. She had dressed quietly and left the bedroom Sandy was using after exactly two hours, saying, 'I am sorry. I have to go. I will get in trouble with Madam Cat.'

He had remained in bed for perhaps another twenty minutes,

he had lost all track of time, looking at the blank magnolia ceiling and trying to imagine her face, her eyes, her body. Then the sounds of movement from elsewhere in the flat infiltrated his mind like a stormcloud. Was it Tom turning in bed, unable to sleep on a humid night, or had May simply moved into Tom's room? Like a bloody railway timetable? He could not bear the thought of her body being so close, yet with someone else. Especially with a man she just might care for in her own way as much as she cared for him, since Tom had been good to her in his own way, even if not good enough. He did not believe she was in her present job because she liked it and wanted to do it. She was in it because it was the only way she could help her brother and her mysterious younger sister, if she had one. He was sure in his own mind that she had one; when she denied it, it was for reasons of her own, whatever they might be.

'Tell me more about your mother,' he had said after the third time.

'There is nothing more to tell.'

'Come on, May, there must be. She was something to do with a fruit farm in mainland China when last you heard of her, wasn't she? Tom said something about it.'

'That was years ago. It does not matter.'

'Of course it matters. It matters just as your young sister matters.'

'I think I go now,' she had said abruptly.

He had laughed and pointed at his wristwatch. 'Still five minutes left of the two hours. Look, perhaps I can help you find your mother.'

She had stopped him talking by getting on top of him and arousing him again. It was all over more quickly this time and afterwards he was exhausted. When she had gone he felt spent and depressed and lost. And now he was having to endure

Tom's attempts at being avuncular and extremely wise.

'Oh, jack it in, Tom. You don't like your Friday night arrangements to be disturbed, that's all.'

'Bollocks. You stand there in your underpants attributing the best motives to her and the worst motives to me. I just don't want you to get hurt, chum, that's all.'

'I'm going to help her find her mother. We talked about it tonight.'

'Don't talk utter balls. She may not have one. Her mother may be dead.' Tom wiped his steaming face with the back of his equally damp hand, which he then waved dismissively. 'Oh, get back to your bloody boat,' he said wearily.

'Ship. Ship! All right, I bloody well will!'

Somehow they were still talking half an hour later, by which time Tom had agreed, if Sandy was still set on it in the cold light of morning, to help Sandy trace May's mother. Tom had added the unreassuring warning, 'You do realise, don't you, that we're both likely to be strapped into the same strait-jacket if things go wrong?'

# 8

'You should not quarrel with your friend,' said May very seriously. 'Not because of me. He is good man.'

Sandy found the overhead light in the centre of the hour-rented hotel bedroom harsh and unsympathetic. It made the crisp pink sheets on the bed, obviously changed just before they arrived over an hour ago, just before sundown, seem even more garish than they were. As May rested on the bed, watching him closely, it threw May's underlip into shadow, as if she had a moustache and made the reflection of his half naked body in the wall mirror look as if it might be made unhealthily of lard.

Sandy struggled into his trousers. 'He is also a very sarcastic man on occasions, and last night was one of the occasions.'

'I know him for a long time, San-di. Next week, the week after that, you will be gone and – '

'I know. I don't want to think about it.'

'You should not worry because you could not . . . It happens, sometimes. It happens more than you would think, San-di, only most men are such liars and they never confess to it, not when talking to their friends. Not all men are as honest as you, San-di.'

'Has it ever happened with Tom?'

'San-di, you do up your trousers and not be naughty. Is against code to talk about clients.'

'I want to be more than a client, May. Don't you know that? I suppose that's the trouble, really. I mean going to a hotel where you pay by the hour, I mean this room, I mean having to pay the woman at the desk in cash when we came in, I mean – '

May suddenly swung her legs off the bed. 'San-di, I do not wish to take your money any more, you spend so much money, but if you not pay me, Madam Cat is angry, my bosses are very angry.'

'I didn't mean that. May, of course I must pay you, if it's the only way I can go on seeing you. I've been on the ship for weeks and weeks, with nothing to spend my money on, so don't worry about the money, because I don't. Five hundred Hong Kong dollars, okay?'

She took the money and pushed it into the handbag which had been beside the bed throughout, as if she did not want to let it out of her sight. 'You are good man, San-di. You must not worry. You be surprised at how many men pay and just want to talk.'

'I didn't just want to talk. May.'

May laughed. 'That I know, San-di. We see each again before you go, it will be all right then, you see.'

'I hope we see each other many many times before I go, May. In fact the thought of not seeing you again . . . '

'You have the buttons of your shirt done up wrong, San-di.'

It was true. He tried to smile and couldn't manage it. He had to undo all the buttons and patiently do them up again. His fingers were trembling and he didn't know whether this was because of confusion or rage at what had happened or to be more exact what had not happened.

A few minutes later he opened the door of the bedroom and stepped back to allow her to go through it first. 'You are nice,' she said and kissed him on the cheek, smiling in a way he could swear was due to pure embarrassment. He found it the most warming and provocative kiss she had ever given him. He took hold of her in the open doorway and kissed her mouth. She wriggled from his grip with a little gasp. He caught up with her at the top of the stairs down to the foyer and reception desk.

'San-di, you look what you do or you fall on top of me.'

'That's what I'd like to do.'

'San-di, that does not sound like my San-di.'

The sound of the possessive word 'my' gave him a thrill, even though he couldn't quite believe, as she made her way expertly down the ill-lit stairs, that she had not said it to a dozen others, perhaps at this very hotel.

As they reached the bottom of the stairs, a young Chinese man in heavy spectacles and a bright yellow suit came through the front door of the hotel, followed by a tall well-built Chinese girl in a vivid red dress cut very low, revealing all of her well fleshed shoulders.

Sandy heard May, walking ahead of him, drew in her breath sharply. The penny dropped. The bright red dress was vaguely familiar. This must be the girl who was making herself objectionable to May because he had no eyes for anyone else.

He put his arm protectively round her shoulder.

The girl in red looked hard at May, and said something to her in Cantonese. Her voice was low and husky, as if she had smoked too many cigarettes. She was smoking one now, having only just come in off the street. As a non-smoker, Sandy did not greatly care for women who smoked in the street, especially when they were obviously making sneering remarks to May.

May answered her, also in Cantonese. Her tone was more high-pitched than usual. Sandy didn't understand a word of it, but the man with the girl in red, who Sandy judged to be about the same age as himself, obviously did. Sandy tightened his grip on May's shoulder and propelled her towards the door to the street. The man and the girl were passing them in the foyer when the man turned back and came towards May, hurling obvious insults in barking Cantonese.

Sandy took his arm from May's shoulder and stood directly in front of her.

He forced himself to draw his lips back in a forced smile. 'Shall we leave this to the ladies?' he said.

Perhaps the girl in red's client did not understand the words, perhaps he understood them and took exception to them. His foot came up from the ground in a wide arc and, if Sandy had not pulled his head backwards without conscious thought, would have connected with his face. As it was, it connected painfully with his shoulder, pushed him backwards and sent him stumbling over May's feet until he fell backwards flat on his back.

With other officers-in-training, he had almost humorously discussed the art of self-defence, but all that discussion had not prepared him for how helpless he felt on the floor, having been attacked without, as he saw it, warning. He was on his feet in a split second – his brother officers had insisted that was crucial in such a situation – but having done that he didn't quite know what to do except place himself in front of May again. This he promptly did, preparing himself for a further onslaught and asking himself whether he should grab the man's attacking arm or leg and pull him off balance or get in first. But get in first with what?

Sandy did not have to make up his mind. While he was standing there certain of only one point – that, whatever happened, whether he had to kill the man or risk being killed himself, he would defend May – the woman behind the reception desk walked round in front of it. She was not unaccompanied. In her hand she carried a meat cleaver, the thin rectangle of shining steel glittering in the light from the fake crystal chandelier.

The man took one look at it and gasped. Then he turned and walked out of the hotel, leaving the girl in red standing staring after him.

Sandy grabbed May's arm and piloted her out of the front

door and into a passing cab before the other woman could pull herself together sufficiently to make trouble.

'San-di, you were wonderful,' said May once they were both in the cab. 'You treat me like no other man, never. What is your great English hero – St George? You were like him, yes.'

'It wasn't all me, though I hope I made him see I wasn't an easy pushover where you were involved. The sight of that meat cleaver seemed to paralyse him. I should have thought he was tougher than that.'

May Fong said nothing.

'I thought he was some sort of martial arts nut and could have easily taken that nasty instrument off her, but he didn't even try.'

May still said nothing.

'Immediately he saw that cleaver, he just turned tail and ran for it. You know any other hour-hire hotels, May? Shall we try another one? I'll pay. I feel in the mood now, by jove, yes. I don't think anything will go wrong this time.'

Two hours later Sandy walked back to the ship, whistling happily to himself. Only one other thing was still on his mind. Why had that man, after making all the waves at the start, given in so easily? Did it matter? Hardly. The fact was that May was safe and May was certainly grateful, to say the least, and showed it. He carried on his silent whistling even after he had reached the wardroom and put on the expected non-committal social expression.

*Part Two*

# 9

1841

The brisk wind was almost dead astern of HMS *War Lion*. It filled her sails and made her masts and yardarms creak, her wooden hull groan. She made almost fifteen knots towards Stanley Fort at the southerly tip of Hong Kong island, her gigantic swishing paddle wheels adding their quota of imperial power.

'Land in sight, sir!'

'Aye. Steady as she goes.'

Captain Wembley, alone on the wooden deck of the bridge, believed fervently in economising in the use of fuel whenever possible. On this occasion the benefits of a speedy triumphal retreat to Stanley Fort over-ruled economy. He was in a hurry to show his spoils to the populace. The advantages of the new engines over sail, however, had not yet convinced him. He saw their high costs of operation militating against the flag rank and knighthood he sought. His job was to protect as many as possible of the trading ships carrying the lucrative poppy, and to do it as economically as possible because there were still some at home who regarded the opium trade with blanket disapproval and would leap at any suggestion that money was being squandered on it.

'Are our piratical friends ready?'

'Aye, sir, chinks ready to be brought up on deck.'

'Good.'

His briefing at the Admiralty before he set off to the Far East was to remember diplomatic necessities as well as military ones. A firm but discriminating hand. This was an occasion for firmness. 1841 was the fourth year of Queen Victoria's reign, and the first year of Hong Kong's addition to the other fortunate parts of the world which, as colonies of the British Empire, were being brought peace, prosperity, education and Christianity. Now the Imperial Chinese Government had achieved some success in driving the British opium trade from the mainland of China, an island base off its coast, like Hong Kong, was obviously a major asset and one worth fighting for.

'A mile to go, sir.' The First Master, Hillcote, stood on the lower deck, below the wheel deck. He had a powerful Devon voice. Facing the enlarging dot that was Stanley Fort, he did not need to turn his head to make himself heard by the captain.

Captain Wembley, too, could make himself heard without a megaphone. 'Prepare the executions, First Master.'

'Aye, aye, sir! I will. We'll deal with 'em. We'll get these murdering chinks ready for a taste of justice.'

'Make sure everyone ashore, including their cronies no doubt, can see 'em, First Master. Give it five more minutes.'

'They'll see 'em for sure, sir, when we string 'em up. I'll see to that.'

'Do so, First Master. You have my leave to carry on at will. Get them on deck now, and string them higher when we're close enough for everyone at Stanley can see. Get a reliable and agile officer to do it.'

'I have one in mind, sir. Britton.'

'Excellent. Proceed.'

The Chinese men were whimpering when Lieutenant Billy Britton brought them up on deck at the end of his cutlass. Their bleeding wrists were tied behind them with thin twine. Their faces had been bruised and cut as they fell 'by accident' at the end of a zealous rating's boot down the steep ladders down to the lower decks. They had been in the hot windowless cubicles by the aft mast for five days. Billy Britton had supervised their incarceration. Billy Britton was what his fellow officers called him to his face, though it often changed to Bully Britton behind his back. Ordinary seamen used the less sympathetic version all the time.

'Keep moving there, you heathens!' shouted Billy Britton. 'You waiting for your gods to save you? Not a hope. We're going to give you a better view of Hong Kong than you've had in your lives! Something others will remember, if you don't! Not so brave now as when you were murdering unarmed British merchantmen, are you? Keep moving!'

The five pirates, who between them had seized three British merchant ships carrying profitable poppy and killed all the crews, were dressed in shapeless dark shirts and trousers. All had 'lost' their sandals; their feet were bare, cut and filthy. Their matted hair was full of lice. Their eyes were blank with terror. Captain Wembley watched them without a shred of pity as they made their way for'ard, goaded by Billy Britton's cutlass. Trade was trade. The opium trade between China and parts of the British Empire such as India was good business, everyone must know that by now. Some Chinese said the opium was to degrade the Chinese and Indians. Rubbish. It was to make them happy. If it didn't make them happy, at least it kept them quiet, which was the main thing.

'Watch that young chink, Lieutenant Britton!' Hillcote pushed himself up on the balls of his feet to make himself taller. He always wore the double breasted jacket with the wide lapels and the epaulettes, as First Masters were entitled to do when acting as executive officers. Few other officers did. They preferred the more informal and easily put-on single breasted jacket, with its ten large buttons from wait to throat which effectively concealed dirty linen. Slovenliness! Lack of ambition. Hillcote hated it, and wished the captain would do something about it. 'Don't press 'em too hard. First Master,' was all he could get out of the captain on the subject.

Billy Britton shouted back at the First Master: 'Aye, aye, sir, I'll attend to the lively one!'

The running Chinese man was the youngest of the group. All Chinese men, except the very old, looked like naughty schoolboys to Billy Britton; this one looked like a very naughty schoolboy indeed. He ran back towards the stern of the ship on the port side. Billy Britton took the starboard side, headed him off and stopped him by thrusting his cutlass between the running brute's legs. The man screamed as he crashed down on to the deck, blood streaming from his legs. A seaman standing nearby hauled him to his feet and dealt him a blow across the face with a fist.

'Cowards, the lot of 'em!' shouted Billy Britton proudly, his cutlass still in his hand. He pushed and kicked the young Chinese back towards his partners, just to teach him a lesson.

Stanley Port was now growing larger by the second. Already the men on the ship could see human forms at the quayside, European as well as Chinese. There was always great interest in the return of one of Her Majesty's warships, especially one with the new steam-driven paddles. It was right that the surrounded minority of British citizens on Hong Kong island should see the results of HMS *War Lion*'s triumph in capturing the pirates, and that the native Chinese should see for themselves the inevitable results of taking up arms against Queen Victoria.

Hillcote liked few of the men aboard. He liked Billy Britton. The young lieutenant with the round face and fair hair might be overweight and no great intellect. But the sight of his naval cap, with the gold braid around the rim always well down over his forehead, so that his eyes were hardly visible, was reassuring. He was invariably well turned-out. 'You're doing well, Britton. Carry on the good work. Murdered Englishmen will rejoice.'

The Chinese had now almost reached the shrouds. At their base was a formation of knotted rope, rather like a vast triangular cobweb that acted as support to the base of the shrouds and also acted as a ladder for crew members going aloft to the yardarms. Billy Britton pointed aloft and made thrusting movements of his cutlass to make it clear that he expected the Chinese to begin climbing. One of them fell on his knees and began to scream in a loud continuous wail ended only by a hard kick from Billy Britton and another from a seaman hoping for promotion.

'That's the ticket, man! Keep them moving.'

Another of the Chinese broke away and headed straight for Billy Britton, his eyes staring, his lips drawn back in a snarl. Britton saw him coming and stood his ground, raising his cutlass at the last moment. Foam on his blue lips, the running Chinese impaled himself on the sword, pulling at it with his hands to make sure it did its work. Britton lowered the tip of his sword, allowing the dead man to slide off it on to the deck.

'Get this one up there first! Carry him up, if you have to! Yes, you, Ferguson, what are you waiting for? You'll do. And Simons. Grab the chink and get him up there and get the rope round his neck so everyone can see him . . . That's the ticket!'

Ferguson and Simons had been watching from behind a capstan. Trouble-makers both, thought Britton. Ferguson was tall and sallow, Simons short and plump. They were often seen in one another's company. Both hesitated, saying nothing. Then they hauled the dead Chinese up the shrouds towards the yardarm, from which five nooses swung at the end of five lengths of thin rope, It took Ferguson and Simons some minutes to get the man's neck into the noose and allow him to drop towards the deck, swinging in the wind, blood trickling down from his legs.

Billy Britton shouted: 'Well done, Simons. Not quite so well done, Ferguson, you were supposed to be hanging him, not waiting to see whether he'd hang himself. Let's do better with the others, shall we?' He knew it was the reverse of the truth: Ferguson had been the leader as always, but leaders in the ranks were better kept in their place.

It had been difficult to get a dead man up to the noose; it proved even more difficult to get the live men up there. The first tugged and pulled as Ferguson and Simons got him near the shrouds.

'Oh, get a grip on him, Ferguson, he's a murdering pirate, not your sweetheart, if you've got a sweetheart. Have you got a sweetheart, Ferguson? Apart from Simons?'

Ferguson almost let go of the arm of the Chinaman as he turned and looked at Billy Britton. 'Yes, sir, I have a sweetheart, and I'm glad she's not hereabouts to see me now.'

Billy Britton could hardly believe his ears, even though it was Ferguson. 'What did you say, man?'

Simons, his face now even whiter with fear as he clung to the Chinese man's other arm, gave his mate a beseeching stare. 'Ferguson, watch yourself,' he hissed.

Ferguson bit his lip. 'I didn't say nothing, sir.'

'Oh yes you did, man. Out with it! Let us all enjoy your profundity. It was a profound remark, I take it?'

Ferguson braced himself on the deck, pulling himself to his full height. The Chinese man they held started to groan and moan. The others started to shout and scream all at once.

'Come on, man, I'm waiting. We're all waiting. I insist you share your wisdom.'

'This is what I said, sir. I said I'm glad she's not here to see me now. Sir.'

'Ah! Yes, you're a clever man, Ferguson. I always said you were a clever man, slightly too clever perhaps. Now kindly tell us why you're glad she's not here to see you hang a few murdering pirates, enemies of the Queen, mark you, by the neck as they richly deserve?'

'She don't like the sight of blood, sir.'

Britton was preparing the way for a charge of treason, no less, and perhaps Ferguson knew that he was, but was too angry to care. 'Oh, no, that won't do, Ferguson. We all know that all ladies dislike the sight of blood. Why wouldn't she like this particular business, if you please?'

'Because she's not a hypocrite, sir.'

Simons pulled at his friend's arm. Ferguson shook him off. He stood a head taller than Britton. His blue eyes were icier, even icier than usual.

Britton said: 'You are indeed ambitious in your choice of Queen's English in which you choose to insult the Queen, Ferguson. Hypocrite? Not a word I would expect from a common seaman. Why hypocrite, if you please? Pray tell us all.'

'We're as bad as they are, sir. That's what I'd think she'd say if she was here. We're as bad as they are. Sir.'

There was a communal drawing in of breath. Then Britton said: 'Your words have been noted. We'll settle this little matter later, Ferguson, shall we? You've given me plenty to go on.' He pointed with his cutlass. 'Get that chink and all the other chinks up there on the yardarm in a trice or I swear to God I'll come behind you with my cutlass and get you up there fast enough. Understood?'

Simons gave another tug at Ferguson's arm. Slowly the taller man blinked, shook himself, and got both hands on the Chinese man again, as if hoping the man would come with no further trouble. The man did not oblige him. He struggled, pulled and tugged and kicked. With the rope already half way over his head, he kicked out even more violently. Both Ferguson and Simons, to stop themselves from falling, had to let go so that they could hold on to the yardarm with both hands. With a scream, the man started to fall. His foot got caught in the dangling noose and as he fell, his ankle snapped. He screamed louder and louder as he swung by the foot above the deck.

'You fine pair! You scrimshankers!' Billy Britton was enjoying himself. 'Get him loose and hang the swine! Hang the swine properly in the name of the Queen! Get it done or I'll come up there myself and both of you will be in irons!'

Two minutes later, Ferguson and Simons were still struggling with the Chinese. The people on the quayside at Stanley Fort were now clearly visible. The ship, now in shallow water where waves were breaking, listed from side to side. The town, its few hastily-constructed towers dominating the more primitive buildings of the shanty area, had turned out in force to see the *War Lion*. Lieutenant Billy Britton started to climb the shrouds as he had warned, his cutlass back in its scabbard. It did not stay there long. He thrust it in the direction of Ferguson rather than the Chinaman once he had got level with them on the yardarm.

'You useless pair! Get him free! You want them to see this shambles from the shore? You want them to think we can't hang five miserable pirates properly? I'll have both of you for this . . . What? Still no action? Then like this, you poor apes . . . '

Lieutenant Billy Britton, twenty-two and in the Royal Navy only because another profession was out of the financial reach of his parents, who kept an hotel in Dorset, hung grimly on to a yardarm rope with one hand and made a thrust with his cutlass, piercing the Chinese man in the chest. Then, using all his strength, he made a great semi-circular sweep with the sword. It severed the man's ankle. The foot fell in gentle circles into the sea, landing over thirty feet from its dying owner.

'Swim to the shore if you can!' said Billy Britton with satisfaction.

Only four Chinese pirates were hanging from the yardarm when HMS *War Lion*, her paddles now spinning idly, drew into Stanley Fort, a sight cheered by the usual assortment of British colonial officials, off duty soldiers, sailors and merchants who welcomed all incoming ships from the quayside. Not all the Chinese on the quay cheered.

With *War Lion* securely tied up, First Master Hillcote, with Captain Wembley's full concurrence, and at Billy Britton's pressing suggestion, put both Ferguson and Simons in solitary confinement for dereliction of duty, claiming they had incompetently conducted the executions, and in doing so had uttered words that insulted the Queen. Captain Wembley ruled out Britton's suggested charge of treason on the grounds that it would be bad for the whole ship, but agreed to his suggestion that Ferguson be kept confined in one part of the ship and Simons in another.

# 10

1841

HMS *War Lion* was due to stay at Hong Kong for seven days. Then it was to return five missionaries to Britain. Cholera had caused the death of one of the missionaries before *War Lion* reached Hong Kong; another was recovering from typhus but would remain too ill to move before the ship's scheduled departure.

There was little to do in Hong Kong except catch one disease or another. The men were advised to stay aboard the ship and to sniff garlic as often as possible, to protect them from the wide range of tropical diseases that would affect at least one in three of the troops and civilians stationed there. Lieutenant Billy Britton was luckier than most. He had a friend in Hong Kong who, unlike many members of the Colonial Service, had not gone down with either cholera or typhus or the less serious but almost equally disabling dysentery.

'Ten tots of rum a day, Billy, that's the ticket,' said Charlie Webster, as the two men talked in Webster's rooms at the temporary Colonial Service compound, well clear of the shanty town. 'Show the fever who's master.'

'Rum? I thought you were a whisky man. Where'd you get rum? Not some fine fiddle at the naval stores?'

'Ask no questions and you'll be told no lies. Is it to your taste?'

'You're a damned rogue, Charlie. One day you'll come to grief.'

'No one but a bit of a rogue would come out to a sewer like

this, Billy, I know that, you know that, they know that. Here I can escape the bills and concentrate on the drink and the girls. Less trouble altogether. The girls are quite willing here if you've a mind; and they don't object to the unusual, if that's your taste. I can testify to that.'

This had been part of their conversation the day HMS *War Lion* reached Hong Kong from the Indian Ocean, barely three hours after the ship had tied up near the wooden-hulled HMS *Tamar*, a much older ship than *War Lion*, which relied totally on her sails. Billy Britton had gone ashore despite the warnings. He always said he believed that if God had marked you down he had, and if he hadn't he hadn't, and that was that. He had gone to the Colonial Service compound, which stood halfway up the hill overlooking the harbour, a respectable distance from the smells and infections at steamy ground level, and found Charlie Webster in a wooden hut almost as big as the hut of the entire medical centre. Charlie, it transpired, shared the hut with the colony's doctor, a pale young man with a nervous tic in his right eye, who swore he was a teetotaller but was somehow always nearby when Charlie found the level in his rum decanter mysteriously low. Often Charlie put the decanter under his steel bed, half for safety and half so that he could reach for it on hot steamy nights and refresh himself, afterwards carefully wiping his dark moustache. Now that Britain had formally signed a treaty with the Chinese, giving Hong Kong island to the British in perpetuity and Kowloon and the New Territories on the mainland for a lease lasting until 1997, rumours had seeped through that the men of the Colonial Service there would soon enjoy amenities taken for granted elsewhere in outposts of the British Empire. So far, nothing much had happened. Even pillows and cotton sheets had not arrived; mosquito nets were in short supply, adding to the chances of catching fevers.

Charlie Webster had gone to the same public school as Billy Britton. Both had followed the same route of misbehaviour, rebellion and expulsion. Charlie was only six months older than Billy, though he always spoke as though it were six years.

'If you have any rum or other libations with you over here, you should keep it with you all the time,' he advised. He motioned Billy to sit down on the vacant bunk normally used by the doctor. 'Otherwise it's a case of the biter bit, if you get my drift. You cadge it from stores; someone else steals it from you. That's the drill. If you have anything valuable, keep it with you all the time. You can't trust the chinks, not an inch.' He took a swig from a hip flask containing rum intended solely for the use of Her Majesty Queen Victoria's navy, and held out the flask to Billy.

Billy waved it away. 'Not that I think you've caught something nasty, Charlie. Anyhow, I always say if you're going to catch something, you'll catch it.'

'Right, Billy. If God's marked you down, he's marked you down. You know why I'm in here with the doctor? No one else would share with him, that's why. Not when he's touching our own crowd who've gone down with something nasty, even touching chinks – only the ones who work for us, of course. The others aren't our affair, thank God. Let them pray to whatever heathen gods they pray to, and see how far that gets them. Usually they die like flies all the same. The Queen!'

Billy watched Charlie downing the rum, his long thin face going redder as the liquid went down his thin throat. He didn't notice the doctor's arrival at first and when he did he got up from the bunk, put hands behind his back in order to avoid shaking hands and, ignoring Charlie's amused look, told him he'd leave him to his stack of papers as he had to get back to the ship.

'Look, you must come aboard before we move on,' he added.

'We're having a party aboard tomorrow for officers, men and their guests. Be my guest. We can talk some more about old times. There'll be women aboard. You can see how Jack Tar behaves in a heathen port.'

'My formal dress is a bit ragged, I'm afraid, I scarcely ever wear it now. Will a tropical suit answer?'

'Oh, you won't need formal gear. It's not that sort of party – at least it won't be after the first two hours. That's when the captain, you can rely on it, will retire with the other top brass to their quarters, determined to hear and see absolutely nothing, and the real party will begin. Arrive at nine. You could even bring a brace of obliging ladies with you, and no one would say a dicky bird. We've been at sea a long time.'

'That sort of party, is it? I'll see what I can arrange. Don't expect me until after nine.'

'Excellent,' said Billy Britton. He nodded affably to the doctor on his way out, but still didn't offer his hand. He saw the little smile on Charlie Webster's face.

# 11

1841

By the next day, the missionary with typhus had died. The one at first thought to have dysentery obviously had something far more dangerous and was now in the Colonial Service compound's medical centre, a wooden hut with ten wooden bunks, where the thin young doctor wiped his face with a damp towel every half hour. The remaining two missionaries were taken aboard HMS *War Lion* for safety's sake and stayed there during that night's party, though they went to their assigned spare officers' cabins at the same time as the captain and his senior officers.

'Don't get bored, Charlie, the interesting part is yet to come,' advised Billy Britton. Already he had drunk almost half a bottle of rum.

The temperature in the wardroom was almost unbearable. In the light of the lanterns swinging from the wooden beams, faces looked as red as lobsters. Billy found it difficult, through the smoke, to focus on the pictures on the wardroom walls: one showing the previous HMS *War Lion*, an all-sail frigate run aground and lost in 1787, another showing a newly-crowned Queen Victoria, looking down on the smoke and the noise with an innocent, enigmatic half smile.

'God, it's hot in here, Billy. No room to swing a cat, either.'

Charlie Webster's speech was beginning to be slurred. It was part of his job to show off the Colonial Service to visiting naval officers, and free drink was not to be despised; but he suffered from catarrh, and all this smoke, though possibly warding off horrible diseases, was bad for his nose.

Billy dug him in the ribs. 'If you think this is crowded, Charlie, you should see how Jack Tar lives on the lower decks. These modern ships are built for speed, not space.'

'Could anything be more crowded than this?'

'Oh yes. I'll lay you odds, Charlie, that Jack is much more crowded one deck down. I'll also lay odds that Jack is having a more lively party. Your common or garden Jack knows how to look after himself on these occasions, believe you me. The Captain doesn't go down there at all on a night like this, you see – Jack wouldn't be glad to see him and he wouldn't be glad to see Jack. Turn a blind eye and all that. Jack just wants to get on with his drink and his women.'

'Women? You mean the men can bring woman aboard?'

'You must know all about this from other ships that have been here, Charlie. The women come aboard themselves and no questions asked, provided there's no trouble. A blind eye is turned.'

'Are you swaying or is it the ship? Is there no fear of the fevers when they allow these women aboard?'

'Put it this way. Her Gracious Majesty might well prefer the lower decks to enjoy their women aboard than go with them to their lice-ridden hovels ashore. As long as they keep them out of sight, of course. If they brought them within sight of the upper decks, that would be a different kettle of fish. Someone would have to do something about it.'

'You surprise me, Billy,' said Charlie seriously. He was determined to get a long look at the lower deck.

'Then follow me, Charlie. No one else will notice. I'm entitled to show a Colonial Service man the ship. You'll see a sight or two, I warrant. Some of the hags who get aboard are old enough to be their mothers – not that you can always tell the correct age with the chinks – but Jack Tar can't afford to be too particular.'

'Why are you getting yourself so excited, then, Billy old chap?'

'If you'd been at sea with nothing to look at except more sea and Chinese pirates for seven weeks . . . Mind your head on the wardroom door, Charlie . . . that's it, down those steps – don't worry, the ship's as steady as the Rock of Gibraltar. In rough weather, going down here can be a bit tricky.'

At the bottom, they were surrounded by stinking barrels oozing salt, obviously once used to hold fish or meat. Billy led the way through the gun deck, its beamed roof so low that they had to stoop as they made their way through bags of powder, piles of cannon balls and stacks of ramrods. Shouting, laughter, thuds and screams were clearly audible.

'What did I tell you, Charlie? See here. They have a better time than we do. Molly-coddled, that's your ordinary Jack today – you know there's even talk of not flogging him any more? They'll not be as silly as that when it comes to the point, of course; you won't keep Jack in his place without a touch of the cat o'nine tails now and again . . . There, what did I tell you?'

The men's quarters was indeed more crowded than the officers' wardroom. The ceiling was lower. The vertical timber ribs of the hull, rough hewn and unpainted, stood out at least three feet. Rough horizontal shelves no more than two feet wide, between the timber ribs, served as the men's bunks. On the bunks and in the far corners some sailors were alone with glasses of rum in their hands; others had Chinese girls with them in various stages of undress.

'This is allowed?' said Charlie Webster. 'With fevers like we see, this is still allowed?'

Billy laughed. 'Of course it's not allowed, Charlie. Not

officially, I should think not. Privately, I think the captain agrees with you, though – if God has marked you down, he has, and if he hasn't he hasn't, and that's the beginning and end of it. Disappointing lot of chink drabs on the whole, aren't they?'

Charlie Webster said, too casually: 'Who's the rather nice one over there?'

'The one with the flower in her hair? I saw her first.'

'Too late. She seems to be with that tall seaman.'

'We'll see about that,' said Billy.

The object of their joint attention was sitting on one of the bunks: a young Chinese girl with shining black hair neatly drawn back into two pig-tails in such a way that her deep fore-head and white oval face were clearly revealed. The flower was at the top of one pig-tail. She was wearing a kimono which had been opened to reveal her firm and ample breasts. The seaman with her on the bunk, his hand inside her kimono, was Ferguson. He had been sentenced to three strokes of the cat o'nine tails, the sentence, for diplomatic rather than disciplinary reasons, to be carried out when they were at sea again.

'Too good for the likes of him, Charlie!' Billy pushed his way through the drinking, singing, swearing seamen towards the girl. Charlie followed, wondering who the girl was, and whether he could find her again ashore if this evening was a wash-out. He was rather alarmed by the men around him, though luckily most seemed too drunk to pay him any attention. At last they reached Ferguson and the girl. Charlie noticed that the girl, unlike many of the others, did not appear to be drunk; her large blue eyes were clear and direct, her red mouth was generous and firm, not a twisted slit like most of the rest. Under their scrutiny she moved slightly away from Ferguson, staring up at them with her clear eyes and pulling her kimono together so that her breasts were no longer on view.

These airs and graces angered Billy. He got hold of her by the wrist, glaring at the tall, sallow-faced seaman. 'You know the rules, Ferguson, and you can't afford any more trouble. You're only out of irons because the Captain's too Christian a man and doesn't understand the depths of depravity of men like you. No under-age girls on the ship at any time. Who is she?'

Ferguson looked up at him from the bunk, trying to focus his eyes. His voice was less befuddled than Billy had expected. 'Her name's May Fong, sir, and she's not under age.'

'You mean she's not under age, Sir! I say she is under age and an officer is the best judge of these things.'

Ferguson sat up straighter on the bunk. He struggled to smooth down his tunic. 'There's a lot of girls here under-aged, then Sir! Why don't you pick on them, too?'

'Don't adopt that tone with me, Ferguson. I say this girl is under age, so she is under age.'

'I'm sorry, sir, if you and the other officers are bored with your own party.'

'Stand up, Ferguson. Hands to your sides. You're too clever, Ferguson, too clever altogether. Perhaps you need a double taste of the cat to teach you respect for officers.'

Ferguson stared down at Billy from his great height. He said nothing. It was Charlie Webster who, after reflecting that his friend Billy Britton might be on shaky ground if it came to an official enquiry, said: 'Can't we forget it, Billy? He didn't mean any harm.'

'You don't know these men like I know these men, Charlie. You don't know this man in particular. Some of these men can be the scum of the earth, like this man here. What are you, Ferguson?'

Ferguson stared at him stonily, his jaw set.

'I said what are you? Answer, man!'

Ferguson's lips twitched into a smile. 'The scum of the earth, sir. Is there anything else you would like me to say? I'll try to oblige, sir. We must keep the ladies entertained.'

Billy went puce. He stared at the taller man for a long time. Then he gave a short explosive laugh. 'You want to oblige, do you, Ferguson? That makes a nice change, I must say. But I won't put you to any trouble. I'll make things easy for you. I'll escort this under age lady off the ship for you, and save you from a touch of the cat – yes, I'll enjoy doing that for you, Ferguson.'

Ferguson leaned forward as if about to launch some sort of attack on Billy. May Fong leaned forward and grabbed Ferguson's hand, as if to save him from himself. That made Billy even angrier.

'You see, Ferguson, even the lady is advising you against rash action. These chinks may not know much English, but they can put two and two together. Would you tell your lady friend to stand up and put her attire in order. Mr Webster and myself will see her safely off the ship. Oh, and Ferguson, one more thing, just to put your mind at rest. You may be quite sure that she will receive the best possible attention from both of us.'

For a moment it looked as if Ferguson might attack the officer despite May Fong's restraining hand. Out of the press of men gathering round, his short, fat friend Simons stepped forward. His voice was as obsequious as ever. 'He's had one or two over the eight, sir. Take no notice of him. I'll look after him.'

'You see, Ferguson? Your friend has far more sense than you have.'

'One day, SIR – '

'Yes, Ferguson, one day? One day? Haven't you thought better of your progressive opinions? Pray continue. You have my ear. You have everyone's ear. Go on, Ferguson, if you dare.'

'One day, sir, things will be different.'

'Is that a threat, Ferguson? Did everyone hear that threat?'

'No, sir, just a prophecy. One day. Not in my time, perhaps, not even my children or grandchildren maybe, but one day things will be different.'

'Most interesting, Ferguson, but you seem to be going round in circles now. We mustn't detain you. You mustn't waste what is obviously a fine mind on the likes of us . . . Come, madam, we're going to see you safely off the ship. We're going to look after you very well indeed.'

Once in his cabin, Billy tossed a coin to decide who would have her first. Charlie Webster called tails, and lost. Billy had her three times, then passed her over to his friend. She didn't want to leave after that, asking for more money, so they went up on deck and pushed her bodily down the gang-plank. She resisted so much they had to manhandle her. In the course of this, she tripped and fell into the harbour.

Both men roared with laughter as they made their way back to Billy's cabin, and roared some more when Billy produced the double-headed penny he had used for the toss. They companionably finished off the remnants of the available rum, still laughing.

*Part Three*

# 12

'It is a man's veracity rather than a bicycle in the harbour which is at issue here, Lieutenant. He deserves that you be very precise indeed about what you saw and didn't see.'

Sandy forced himself to look Lieutenant Commander Hillcote straight in the eye. Eye contact was held to be highly important in these matters. 'I understand that, sir.'

He understood a lot more. He understood that the First Lieutenant of HMS *War Lion*, the man responsible directly to the captain for the discipline of the ship, the man who was hearing the case against Simons concerning the stolen bicycle in the absence of Captain Wembley, who had been called away to Singapore for some sort of ceremonial visit, did not like him one little bit. The doubtful stare he fixed on Sandy was proof of that.

'I am glad you do understand it, Lieutenant. Let us proceed.' He drummed his fingers on the wardroom table as if he would have preferred to be somewhere else, possibly on some official binge in Singapore.

Sandy would also have preferred to be doing something other than giving evidence against Simons about a misappropriated bicycle. It was supposed to his day off, and it could have been if the idiot sailor who was supposed to be within sight of the gangplank at all times had been where he was supposed to be. He needn't have become involved at all.

Hillcote's well-known connections with the nobility had, some spitefully said, helped him get several leg-ups in the Royal Navy and was even expected to get him into or very near the top job. It hadn't done so yet and Lieutenant Commander

Hillcote was not an easy man as a result. His striking, staring grey eyes in a thin intense face told the world that he was not receiving his due, and was determined to know why not and what was to be done about it. He was popular neither with his fellow officers nor the men and, according to one school of thought, had several times been promoted out of trouble. At first he had shown signs of wanting to recruit Sandy as an acolyte in his frictions with Captain Wembley.

'I'd say he's a very . . . large man, wouldn't you say, Sandy?' he had once, early in their acquaintance, asked Sandy of the captain, with a harsh laugh that was supposed to be encouraging but which had alarm bells ringing even in Sandy's unsuspicious head.

'I'd say he was the Captain, sir,' Sandy had replied.

Since then he had been on strictly formal terms with the First Lieutenant of *War Lion*; no first names even in the wardroom, no favours sought or gained. Some, he found, thought Hillcote an unusually diligent and able officer; others were equally certain that he was slightly mad.

Lieutenant Commander Hillcote was small and with a neck like a steel cord and wrists like two rather more thin steel cords. He sat behind the wardroom table shouting at all and sundry who did not speak loudly or clearly to be heard above the sound of the ship's machinery, 'Take that confounded brick out of your mouth,' or, 'Stop mumbling and bring the accused in.'

Simons appeared between two seamen, twisting his cap in his hands, a dumpy lump of white-faced bewilderment and innocence. 'Someone has explained your rights to you?' demanded Lieutenant Commander Hillcote.

'Aye, aye, Sir,' said the Master at Arms, a chief petty officer with a red beard and steel spectacles.

Sandy would have preferred it if the Master at Arms, a man with common-sense, were hearing the case, but it would not have been thought suitable when an officer was to be among those giving evidence on which he could be cross-examined.

'Good, good,' said Lieutenant Commander Hillcote. He glared at Sandy. 'Right, Lieutenant. What did you actually see?'

'I was walking back towards the ship, sir, and it was near the harbour gates when Simons overtook me on a bicycle. He was questioned a long time at the gate, with the result that I walked ahead of him again. He overtook me on the bike and I saw him dismount when the reached the gang-plank of HMS *War Lion*, pick up the bicycle and throw it into the harbour.'

Lieutenant Commander Hillcote's protruding grey eyes bored into him. 'Threw the bicycle, you say? Threw it?'

'That's right, sir.'

'No doubt about it?'

'None, sir, I'm afraid.'

'No one need to be afraid, Britton, as long as he reports what he saw and no more than what he saw. There was in your view no chance that it could have fallen in by accident?'

'No, sir. He picked it up and threw it. I formed the impression that he had had too much to drink.'

'We'll leave your impressions and concentrate on what you actually saw, Lieutenant. All right, let's hear the man himself.'

Simons eyes were shifty. 'If I'm entitled to a defence representative, sir, could I have Ferguson? He's waiting outside.'

'You'll have the officer assigned to you. Ferguson's giving evidence later, isn't he? Well then, he can't be your representative or anyone else's. All right, tell us in your own words what happened last night.'

Simons licked his fat pink lips. 'Well, sir, I'd had a bit of beer that night, and you know how it is, sir, it was later than I thought and I don't understand the buses, and I saw this bicycle leaning against a wall in a side street in Wanchai, and I thought the owner wouldn't miss it for a few hours, sir, and I – '

'You're telling us you would have given it back? How would you have managed that?'

Simons did some more lip-licking. 'I didn't think, sir. But theft is wishing permanently to deprive the owner of something, sir, and I didn't intend that.'

If Hillcote privately agreed with Sandy that this performance had been dreamed up in advance with Ferguson, he didn't show it. 'Go on, Simons.'

'Well, sir, I was a bit unsteady, I suppose, and as I got off the gangplank I stumbled a bit and in trying to save myself I let go of the bike, and it went into the drink, sir. If I hadn't let go, I'd have been in the drink myself, sir.'

Sandy thought it was all too trivial; apparently no one had reported a missing bicycle, which may well have been stolen by its previous user, and Simons and Ferguson had not been so disrespectful of him as an officer that action was unavoidable. He was thinking about May Fong when he suddenly realised that Lieutenant Commander Hillcote was talking to him and drumming his fingers on the table. 'I said you have heard what this man says, Lieutenant, is it possible?'

'I'm afraid not, sir.'

'Why?'

'Because I saw him physically pick the bicycle up, at least three feet above the ground, before throwing it into the water, sir. Did the man supposed to be on the gangplank really see nothing?'

'We'll deal with him later,' said Hillcote. 'One thing at a time. This is a case of your word against that of the man himself and that of his one witness.'

'I see, sir. You mean Ferguson confirms Simons' story? I find that hard to believe.'

'Do you now? We'll hear from him in due course. Simons, why was it so crucial that you "borrowed" the bicycle in the first place?'

Simons wrung his hands together. 'You're a fair man, sir. I'd better tell you the truth.'

'Usually the best procedure, yes. Go on.'

'Well, sir, I came across this girl in a bar in Wanchai and she took me to her room and then afterwards I found my wallet was missing, and of course she denied it, but I was left to get back to the ship with no money for a taxi. Well, my blood was up and I admit I borrowed this bike from the front of the place where she'd taken me, intending to return it next day, but I was a bit unsteady on my feet, sir, and when I was halfway up the gank-plank with the bike I tripped and let go of it and it fell into the water, accidentally. That's all there was to it, sir.'

Sandy looked hard at his feet during this evidence. Simons' bar girl sounded a frightful bitch. He was sure that May was not like that at all. He wanted to tell someone this, and hear their agreement, but there was no one to tell. No, May was not like Simons' girl at all – if there had been a girl. Knowing Simons, it was quite possible that Ferguson and he had cooked up the whole story between them.

'I think you'll find, sir,' Sandy heard Simons saying, 'that Ferguson will back up what I'm saying.'

Lieutenant Commander Hillcote suddenly said: 'Lieutenant, did someone say something funny?'

Sandy tried to get May out of his mind. 'No, sir.'

'I thought not. Well, we'd better hear Ferguson.'

Ferguson came into the cabin looking so self-effacing and respectful that it was positively comic to anyone who knew him on a day-to-day basis, as Sandy did and Lieutenant Commander Hillcote didn't. More and more, Sandy wanted to chuck this rubbish and get to the Hot Cat Club or on to the streets of Wanchai, anywhere where he might see her.

Ferguson twisted his cap in his hands. He might have been a

dog humbly waiting to be fed. His tone was pious. 'The officer is quite right, sir – up to a point.'

Hillcote said: 'I'm glad to hear it. But what point is that, pray?'

Ferguson looked full at Sandy. 'Well, sir, Simons had had a few, as I expect most of us had.'

'Are you suggesting,' asked Lieutenant Commander Hillcote, 'that Lieutenant Britton was drunk?'

'Oh no, sir, not at all, I am sure the Lieutenant can handle his drink.'

'And could you handle yours? Had you also been drinking, Ferguson? If so, how much?'

'I may have had a couple of whiskies or so with a friend, sir.'

'One or two, eh? All right, Ferguson, get on with it.'

'Well, I expect you're only interested in what happened inside the harbour gates?'

'Correct.'

'I was walking behind Lieutenant Britton, sir, when Simons overtook us both on a bicycle. He dismounted at the foot of the gang-plank, sir, climbed it and then sort of stumbled. He tried to save the bike, sir, but he couldn't, and the next thing, the bike fell into the harbour.'

'Fell?'

'Oh, yes, sir.'

'The officer says your friend Simons threw it in.'

Ferguson's pitted face cracked into a reverent smile. 'I can understand him thinking that, sir, things happened a bit fast.'

'You're saying the officer is lying?'

'Bless my soul, no sir,' said Ferguson, far too crafty to challenge an officer head-on. 'Simons had got hold of the bike, sir and it rose in the air as he stumbled, so it could have looked to the officer as if he was trying to throw it away, sir. But I was watching him all the time, sir, seeing that Simons is a bit of a mate of mine.'

'Close enough for you to lie for him?' said Sandy.

Ferguson didn't answer. Sandy immediately realised he had made a mistake. Lieutenant Commander Hillcote glared at him. 'I am conducting this hearing, Lieutenant, not you. Ferguson, are you telling the truth?'

'I am, sir. I make no secret of being a bit of a mate of Simons'. But I'm still just telling you what I saw, sir, and only what I saw. Knowing Simons, my guess is that when he took that bike, he meant to return it the next day. He wouldn't need it on the ship, would he, sir? But I can understand the officer making an honest mistake, sir. He was naturally looking for the man who should have been on the gangplank, sir, whereas I was watching Simons all the time.'

'Thank you. Lieutenant Britton, do you wish to modify anything you have said?'

Sandy could see he was getting into deep water because of this little episode. The lower decks would soon be buzzing with well-tailored anecdotes about his disgusting persecution of Simons and Ferguson. She might be at the Hot Cat Club, or walking the streets of Wanchai before going there and he wanted to be there, not here.

'No, sir. I have to stand by what I said.'

'You just might have been mistaken?'

'I might have been mistaken, sir, anyone might be mistaken about anything, but I don't think I was. In fact, I know I wasn't.'

The glare he got in return was glacial. 'Very well,' said Hillcote abruptly. 'Clear out, all of you, while I have a word with the Master At Arms.'

Five minutes later they were all back in the wardroom to hear that the charge against Simons had been proved, that he was due to do two weeks of double special duties – which meant cleaning and other undesirable jobs in his off-duty time – and was also to receive a reprimand which would be entered in his personal record. On the way out, Ferguson smiled an un-pleasant smile at Sandy just as Lieutenant Commander Hillcote called the junior officer back.

'The word of an officer, Britton,' he said once Ferguson and Simons were well out of earshot, 'is never to be seen as being taken lightly, or things might have been rather different. Is that point taken? By the way, how many drinks had you had?'

'Not enough to affect my judgment or my eyesight, sir.'

'I'm glad you're so sure on that point . . . Where do you think you're going?'

'I thought you'd finished with me, sir.'

'Pull yourself together, Britton. Have you got a massive hangover or is your mind somewhere else? We now have to hear the seaman who you say wasn't in full view of the plank, as he should have been. He seems sure that he wasn't out of sight for more than thirty seconds at most.'

'That may well be so, sir. They just happened to be the wrong thirty seconds.'

'You can say that again, Lieutenant. This is quite a morning. I hope your relations with non-commissioned ranks are generally good and will take the strain.'

The man who should have been on the gangplank also got a reprimand and two weeks of double special duties. He claimed he had been out of sight for fifteen seconds at most. His avoidance of Sandy's eyes was more unnerving than the insolence of Simons and Ferguson.

'Well, Britton,' said Lieutenant Commander Hillcote at last, 'this has been quite a morning. It's one way of making a reputation, I suppose. If any of this gets out, it won't do our relations with the Chinese any good, will it? It's all very touchy just now, without this sort of thing.'

The unfairness of it all was too much for Sandy. 'I don't see what else I could have done, sir.'

'You don't see, that the trouble. Or rather, you do see when it would be better not to see. Or am I simply wasting my breath?'

When Sandy at last left the ship, over an hour later, and walked towards the tailors shops of Queens Road East, he was in deepest gloom. He had done himself no good at all, but what else could he have done? Look the other way while Queen's Regulations were being flouted? Hillcote couldn't seriously mean that, surely. Every minute of the wretched business had taken away a minute he could have been looking for May Fong in Wanchai, perhaps seeing her shopping or doing ordinary things that she must do before going to the Hot Cat Club. In that way he would find out more about her, find out what sort of girl she really was under the protective and, he was sure, thoroughly misleading make-up.

He was in a rotten mood because of a trivial bicycle, but at least it had been sorted out and he had seen and heard the last of the whole distracting business.

He was again gravely mistaken.

# 13

He spotted her, at last, at a fruit stall in Lockhart Road, one of the busy streets at the centre of Wanchai near Harbour Road. May did not see him as she fingered some vegetables with slender ivory hands before haggling with the stall-holder, a young Chinese with many silver teeth, and then handing over some money.

Sandy's heart had begun to thump the moment he finally found her. He had spent the remainder of the morning and half the afternoon walking the streets of Wanchai in the hope of finding her, getting more and more irritable as he walked. After leaving the ship, he had waited at a taxi rank behind a queue of what he took to be, despite the civilian clothes, Army squaddies and their girlfriends. The men wore floral silk shirts, black trainer bottoms and thick black boots. The girls wore broad-shouldered black jackets and floral silk floppy slacks. An old stooping Chinese with a straggly beard and battered straw hat had passed the queue and one of the Army idiots had mimicked his walk, the girls giggling loudly, the squaddie doing the impersonation growing even more grotesque. The worst part was that the old man looked back, and must have guessed that the laughter was at him.

'You're a damned disgrace, even for the army!' snapped Sandy.

'Eh?' said the man. 'We're not in the army, you creep. We're British tourists. What's it to you?'

'Nothing. Just as long as you aren't in the navy, that's all.'

'Oh piss off, creep.'

People like them were one of the reasons the locals were

already taking down the pictures of the Queen that had featured prominently in restaurants and public buildings, leaving tell-tale discoloured rectangles on walls, even if most of the pictures in public buildings were still there. Sandy managed not to tell these silk-shirted louts what he thought. He felt it was quite a triumph.

The more he walked, the gloomier and more lost – in every sense – he felt. A lot of what Tom had said last night had been honest and well meant, but that didn't stop him thinking about her – and regarding the presence of some of the more obnoxious Brit civilians as an insult to her personally. The low clouds scudding around the tops of the tall buildings of the Central district made the Mandarin Hotel, the Connaught Centre and City Hall look like forlorn decapitated giants. When at last it began to spurt soft rain, he walked into the nearest restaurant and ordered himself some noodles, which was all he could fancy. Above the bar which ran along one side of the restaurant there was an unfaded rectangle where the Queen's portrait had been.

When the rain stopped as abruptly as it had begun, he decided to cheer himself up by walking towards Queens Road and the tailor's shop where a few days ago he had been measured for a lightweight jacket. At Wah Sun's he picked up the jacket, which fitted perfectly. He put it on and said he would carry his old jacket. He was measured for a pair of cream lightweight trousers, and decided to stroll in a casual way back to Wanchai. Instead he found himself hailing the first cab that caught his eye.

Looking at her unseen as she bought her vegetables, he felt great happiness. His reasoning had been correct: she would sleep late and do her shopping in the afternoon before going to the Hot Cat Club in the evening. He had never thought her merely pretty and now he saw she was beautiful. Beautiful and sad. Without make-up, her face looked rounder and more child-like. She purchased the vegetables and put them into her raffia shopping basket with the concentration of a guileless child, as if nothing else in the world existed but what she was doing at the moment. The top of her yellow silk pyjama suit revealed the sharp points of her far from childlike breasts.

He was less than a hundred feet from her and she was still quite unaware of him. He strode forward, then stopped. She had told him that her apartment was 'not suitable'. Did that mean she was reticent about how she lived? If she looked round and saw him, would she really be pleased – as her time with him had indicated she would be – or would her smile be purely professional? What if she were not pleased? What if she thought he had been spying on her? Any hope he had of getting close to her as a human being would be sunk with all hands. Now he had found her, he didn't know what to do. He was glad Tom wasn't around to observe him and his predic-ament. He couldn't have stood one of his cynical remarks.

As she walked away from the vegetable stall, Sandy followed her without getting closer. She turned into Luard Road and then left again into Hennessy Road, a main thoroughfare of Wanchai which continued eastwards through shops, stalls and offices until it became Yee Woo Street and reached Victoria Park. May was surely not intending to walk that whole distance? She walked very slowly, as if absorbed in her own thoughts; often stopping to look at a stall. Often she reached behind her to adjust one of her two rebellious little pigtails which he had not seen before: her hair at the Hot Cat Club looked altogether more sophisticated. He preferred the pigtails.

At one stall she smiled broadly: he could see her suddenly animated expression even at this distance. The stall was devoted to soft toys. She picked up a two-foot long white turtle and laughed. He only had to stride forward, take it from her, pay for it, and then hand it back to her. But he didn't. While he was hesitating, she reluctantly put the soft white turtle down.

Following her, Sandy quickly picked up the turtle from the stall, paid the surprisingly high asking price without haggling, and waved aside the offer of a paper bag. Immediately he moved on, he wished he had accepted the offer. People stared at him and the giant white turtle under his arm and the last thing he wanted to be was conspicuous.

She did not look back, not even when she crossed busy Fleming Road, when a sideways glance to make sure the nearest traffic was far enough away might have been expected. She behaved as if she did not know he was there; but did she? Had she looked at the turtle deliberately, so that he would do just what he had done, buy it for her? No! It was a rotten unworthy thought. Was there much difference between his suspicion and the attitude of the Brits at the cab rank who had mocked the old Chinese because they didn't regard him as a human being with human feelings? She had been fascinated by the turtle, that was all. The simple explanation was the best: she had simply not seen him, had picked up at the turtle because she had liked it and put it down again because she couldn't afford it.

Sandy followed her through all sorts of streets he didn't know, allowing himself to fall further back in case she turned, until he had lost his sense of direction completely. He would guess they were heading towards the harbour rather than away from it, but he wasn't certain. The concrete walls of the surrounding tenements were uninviting. Sandy was silently sympathising with the people who had to live in them when suddenly she disappeared into one of the open doorways.

At first he wasn't even sure which one, they all looked so much alike. Then he decided it must be the one he had now reached, which appeared to lead to an open wooden staircase. It was dim in the small communal hall. He missed his footing on the first flight of stairs. Above him he could hear her gentle footsteps come to a halt. He froze until they resumed again, when he mounted more steps. Had he done right in coming here? Would she resent it? His feet carried him forward despite his doubts.

By the time he had reached the landing three floors up, he had lost her. There were no footsteps ahead any more. There were no windows and the dim uncovered electric bulb showed him very little. It was so dim he could hardly see either of the two doors directly in front of him. He stood there, breathing hard, the white turtle beginning to slide from his arm. She must have gone into one of the two doors, but which one? He was beginning to feel like a spy. It was not at all a nice feeling. He was about to turn away, reconciled to handing her the turtle in more public circumstances at the Hot Cat Club that evening, when he heard the little scream. It was her voice and it seemed to come from the nearest of the two facing doors.

He tried that door, still clutching the turtle.

The door was unlocked. He pushed it open and found himself in a small room with whitewashed concrete walls and little more than a narrow steel bed, a metal table and two chairs. May was standing near the table, hand pressed against her mouth. A young Chinese in a light blue suit was sitting in one of the chairs, as if he were familiar with the dingy room and had been patiently waiting there for some time. A large meat cleaver of the sort used to chop up ducks in restaurants was on the table, near his hand.

When May saw Sandy she screamed again. He could not tell whether it was relief or fear. The young Chinese jumped to his feet, grabbed the meat cleaver and started brandishing it from side to side in front of him. The second of the steel chairs was in Sandy's hands before he consciously thought about it. The white turtle rolled unheeded to the floor.

The sound made by the Chinese was hardly more than a hiss exclamation he had heard often in Hong Kong, if not with such violence. 'Ha!' Still swinging the meat cleaver from side to side in front of him, he advanced towards Sandy.

May screamed a third time, shouted something in Cantonese and gesticulated wildly. Sandy realised he was standing between the man and the door. He also realised that though he might succeed in holding the man off, he couldn't possibly, unarmed as he was, overcome him. He moved out of the way of the door and in a semi-circle round the table as the other man moved round the other side of the table, still slicing the air with the cleaver.

Only when he was standing directly in front of May did Sandy stop, now holding the chair as a protection for them both but making no sudden movement that could be seen as the forerunner of an attack. The man in the light blue suit saw his chance and ran swiftly to the door. He disappeared down the staircase outside the room, his running footsteps like small arms fire.

Sandy put down the chair. He went to put his arms round May but she avoided him, beginning to cry. He picked up the turtle and handed it to her.

'For you,' he said. 'What was all that about?' He stuttered and his hands were shaking.

May came towards him. He reached out his arms again. She pushed him away violently, then changed her mind and threw herself on his chest, sobbing with equal violence. He held her for a long time until her trembling had stopped. He began kissing her. It was not long before she led him towards the narrow steel bed.

# 14

She lay beside him for a long time, her dark head on his chest, their legs intertwined. He kept his arm round her and with the other hand stroked her hair. He was exhausted. She had seen to that. Despite the barrenness of the room and the hum of the passing traffic, he would have been happy to lie there together in silence for hours, but his questions about the man with the meat cleaver had not been satisfactorily answered.

'May, who was it?' he tried again. 'You can tell me.'

'I do not know, San-di,' she said, pressing her face into his chest. It was impossible for him to see her eyes.

'Look, I can hardly believe you don't know. Why don't you trust me?'

'I do not know, San-di. A robber. Yes. Someone who comes to steal.'

He couldn't say that there was nothing visible worth stealing. 'A robber who comes to steal gets on with it. He doesn't wait for his victim to come home, and he certainly doesn't sit there staring at his meat cleaver on the table.'

'San-di, there are bad men in Hong Kong. You cannot understand our life here.'

Her face was so tightly pressed into his chest that he could now hardly hear her. Gently he turned her face so that he could see her beautiful distressed eyes. 'I can't understand it if you don't explain, that's for sure. Trust me.'

For a brief moment she smiled. She reached out and touched his cheek with a slender, whiter than ivory, forefinger. Her nails were devoid of the red polish she used at the club. Then she turned her head away again. She looked out of the window at the black concrete wall of the next tenement. 'San-di, I do trust you. I know that deliberately – is that the word? – you would never hurt me.'

'Hurt you?' He clasped her more tightly to him. 'Of course I would never hurt you. What made you say such a thing?'

'And I do not wish you to be hurt, San-di.'

'I can take care of myself. May. They really put you through it at naval college, you know. They have self-defence courses there, pretty tough ones. I was quite good at it. What are you laughing at?'

'Oh, San-di you do look so serious and you do talk such strange things. You are so, so innocent about some things, things that I have known since I was a child – '

That nettled him. 'Was that man some sort of gangster? I'm not as innocent as all that, damnit!'

She pushed her face back into his chest. She reached up, found his lips and put a finger across them. 'It is better that you do not ask questions, San-di. It is better that I do not answer them, even if I know the answer. Believe me, please.'

'You have just answered the question, I think. So why was he here?'

'Do not concern yourself, San-di. You can do nothing. He is just . . . a man I know at the club. Yes. He say that I rob him while he sleeps, which is not true. You know I do not do a thing like that.'

'I know. That's why I don't believe what you say. I think you're telling frightful porkies. It wasn't something like that he came for. Look, I'll make it easy for you. I imagine a world like yours has a lot of parasites and hangers-on. People trying to extract money for protection, that sort of thing. Was he one of those?'

'Protection?'

'Come on, May, you know what I'm talking about. People

who say they will damage the club or you personally unless you pay them money.'

'We do not talk of such things. If gentlemen who come to club hear of such things, they go away fast, they do not come to club, so I cannot pay my brother and . . . No, we do not talk about such things.'

'Well, I'm beginning to learn about such things and certainly I'm not going to run away, whatever the rest decide to do. Look, May, have you thought about chucking this life altogether?'

He thought she was crying but she was laughing. 'How long before you back to your ship, San-di? And how long before your ship sails away from here? A week? Two weeks? After that, I have to live here. You are not proposing marriage with me so I get a British passport, are you? Are you?'

The point had arrived too quickly. 'I, er . . . well, I suppose not . . . A bit cynical for me.'

'You see?'

'I didn't mean – '

She silenced him again with the finger across his lips. 'Make love to me again, San-di. Take me again. In any way you like – anything.' She swung away from him and opened her legs.

Yes, her question had caught him unawares and left him feeling a sham – just another western liberal ashamed of the past but not willing to do much about it except soft-talk about the British Imperial past.

'Look,' he said, 'it's all very well for you to say I talk strange things. It's what you said about Tom Webster, too, you know? The first time we were together. You have all these bits and pieces you say to people.' He wanted to sound justly aggrieved but knew he sounded merely plaintive.

'San-di, why do you say these cruel things to me now?'

'Oh god, May, I'm sorry, it's not your fault. None of it is. We're neither of us entitled to talk much about trust, are we?'

That was all he had a chance to say before she swung herself over him. 'You do talk such strange things, San-di. You be quiet now, for me, please.'

It was two hours later that he walked out on to the streets of Wanchai. Street lights were coming on in the suddenly gathering dusk. He had almost forgotten that he had still received no satisfactory answer about the man with the murderous meat cleaver. He could remember only the feel of her and the smell and taste of her, her small pleading voice saying repeatedly, 'San-di, San-di, San-di!'

He was only vaguely aware of the big black car with smoked glass windows waiting at the kerb a few feet away. He moved casually towards the wall to avoid the car's back door as it began to open. Sandy was still not fully aware of what was happening as the very large Chinese chauffeur in immaculate grey livery got out of the car on the other side, moved round the front of the car and stood directly in front of him, first barring his way and then forcing him back against the open rear door. A strong hand from inside the car grabbed his wrist, the chauffeur gave him a hard push in the back and Sandy half staggered, half tripped into the back of the car. The next second the chauffeur was back in the driving seat and the car moved quickly away from the pavement.

Not knowing what to expect next, but fearing that it might well have something to do with meat cleavers, Sandy fumbled for the back door handle. He was unfamiliar with the mechanisms of Rolls Royces and could find nothing that resembled a common or garden door handle or window winder.

A large yellow restraining hand was placed gently on his shoulder from within the car. He saw a thick gold signet ring with an inset jewel, and turned very slowly to find out who was wearing it.

# 15

After no more than a few hundred yards, the big black car stopped in a dead-end street between two concrete buildings. Dustbins and skips of rubbish faced them, washing hung from windows on either side of them.

Sandy felt again for the door handle, and again couldn't find it. 'Look here – ' he began.

'You are in no danger, Lieutenant Britton.' The voice had a thick, guttural Cantonese accent. 'I am sorry that you did not immediately recognise me. We met in the presence of a mutual acquaintance on Saturday night at the Peak. Yes, I am Mr Hok.'

Sandy now had no doubt of this. The face was unmistakable. 'Would you mind letting me out, please? Or do you want an international incident?' Even to him his voice sounded too nervous to be taken seriously.

At last he found the door release. He began to open the car door.

'Certainly you may get out at any time you like, but I think when you hear what I have to say you may wish to remain.' Mr Hok released his grip on Sandy's shoulder. His suit this time was grey chalk stripe. But Mr Hok was plainly the same man he and Tom had seen with May on Saturday night. 'You may leave at any time you wish, Lieutenant Britton. You may be wondering what I want with you. I will tell you that the matter affects the happiness and safety of this mutual acquaintance, the one you know, in European fashion, as May Fong. There! I will push the door even more open. Do you wish to use it?'

Sandy hesitated, his hand on the white leather-lined open door of the Rolls Royce. 'If you harm her . . . ' he began, but the words dried up as Mr Hok laughed. 'How do you mean,' he began again more cautiously, taking his hand away from the door. 'How do you mean, happiness and safety?'

'I do not mean that her happiness and safety will be in any way injured by me, quite the reverse. If we are to talk more, please, we talk with the door closed, yes? Ha!'

Sandy had pulled the door shut. He could manage that with certainty, even in a Rolls Royce. The whole business with the door had been ridiculous. It was, after all, unlikely that a well-off and obviously worldly Hong Kong Chinese businessman would want to be involved in any trouble over an officer of the Royal Navy in the sensitive run-up to the Chinese takeover.

'Ha!' said Mr Hok again. 'That is all I wished to know: your feelings. Please to shake hands, Lieutenant Britton. You are courageous man. The English, as they say, are cool. So! She cares for you. That is easy for her – you are a handsome young man with money to spend. But I see you care for her, too. That is good, very good. If I had to offer you money, I could not trust you.'

It was Sandy's turn to laugh. 'You couldn't trust me? I can't say I care whether you trust me or not. The question I'm asking, Mr Hok, is whether I can trust you. You seem to know a lot about me but I don't know you. I know you only as Mr Hok, the way you introduced yourself on Saturday night. Is that your real name?'

'Mr Hok is good enough. Everyone, they know me as Mr Hok. Mr Hok is good enough on Hong Kong island, Kowloon, the New Territories, in China itself.'

'I dare say.'

'You have not heard of Mr Hok?'

'I've heard you have your fingers in quite a lot of pies.'

'Ha! Your friend Mr Webster filled you in. Good. Yes, many pies.'

'Perhaps protection and bar girls are among them?'

Mr Hok made a dismissive chopping movement with one powerful and well manicured hand. He reached inside his immaculate jacket and produced an alligator hide cigar case. He offered the case to Sandy, who waved it away, and then selected a cigar for himself. He took a gold Dunhill lighter from a waistcoat pocket and lit the cigar, betraying his nebulous origins only by leaving the band on the cigar, which Sandy understood no Englishman of breeding would have done. A slight sheen of perspiration covered Mr Hok's wide forehead. His small black eyes were watchful.

'You are a naval man, Lieutenant Britton; you like to get to the point. There are many engaged in such trades as you mention, but I'm not one of them. Ask your friend Mr Webster.'

Sandy allowed himself to slide further back into the white leather, though not completely convinced that there was no danger to himself. 'Really? I'm glad to hear it.'

'I too have great respect for Miss Fong, and I shall be in Hong Kong rather longer than you. You would like to see her make an end of her present way of life? You care enough about her for that?'

'Yes. I see you haven't talked her out of it yet.'

'I have the power of money, I have not got the power of youth. Your position, I believe, is quite the reverse. Your ship will disappear from Hong Kong in a matter of days, I think. In the meantime, she would listen to you. I would free her from that life, but she will not agree to my terms. Ha! You are beginning to understand.'

'I see.' He certainly wanted May free of her present life but not in order to become the property of an old man like Mr Hok. 'Yes, I am beginning to understand.'

'Do you not think that five years with me, guaranteed, would be better for her than her present life? That is, if you really care for her? Be realistic, Lieutenant Britton.'

'Your terms would rather exclude me, I think.'

'You will be excluded in any case. You will be excluded by several thousand miles of sea. You help free her, you gain her gratitude, your stay here would be very pleasant and, who can say, you might have a chance sometime in the future, if things go wrong between her and me. You see I talk bluntly. Shall we say that, for you, that question is a gamble. We Chinese know how to gamble. Do you?'

So that was it. Mr Hok was not only testing how genuine his feelings for May were, he was giving him a possible future advantage in return for his help now. But what possible help could he be to Mr Hok?

'Let's concentrate on my feelings for May . . .'

'By all means. If her departure from her present life is not handled with . . . tact and foresight, she might be in personal danger. She might be threatened. I do not exaggerate. You may not know of such things, but in Hong Kong such matters have to be carefully considered.'

A chill hand grasped Sandy's heart. 'You've been watching me, I think. There was a man there when I got there, a man with some sort of meat axe.'

'I know him. He is dangerous, but he is a small cog; there are those far more dangerous than he. I can provide her with protection, while I place the right money and perhaps the right favours in the right hands. It is loose ends which I fear, loose ends through which she could be threatened now or in the future. She has a family. A family is a hostage to fortune. A mother on the Chinese mainland and a brother in Hong Kong.'

'And a younger sister in Hong Kong?'

Mr Hok shrugged his shoulders. 'Perhaps. Perhaps. I can

handle the brother, I have contacts in the police and the judiciary. Let us concentrate on the mother. May does not know exactly where her mother is or what she is doing now in China. Now shouldn't a girl be re-united with her mother, Lieutenant Britton?' Mr Hok held up three stubby fingers of his right hand. 'If we achieve this, we achieve a triple benefit. First, she is happier. Second, we are both her heroes. Third, we can see to it that the mother is made aware of the situation and, if necessary, is protected against any actions by criminal elements.'

'Yes, Mr Hok, I can see you can gamble and you can think ahead. Can't you just pay off her employers and leave it at that?'

'I could, yes; others have done that. I have also heard of attempts afterwards to extract even more money. Threats to the girl concerned and to her family have been made in such cases. The mother must be found, re-united with her daughter and warned.'

'How do we do that? I haven't a clue about where her mother is.'

Mr Hok relit his cigar and drew on it in an intense way. 'I have informants in mainland China, many informants. Her mother is in some sort of commune near Canton. I understand that fruit is grown there. There are several such farms, but I know the likeliest. I know more than that.'

'So why haven't you found her, if you're that well informed?'

'This information reached me only yesterday. There are reasons why I cannot act on it personally, reasons why it would be unwise for me to go into communist China at this point. You suffer no such disadvantage. I would of course cover all your out of pocket expenses. Take her to her mother, tell her all she needs to know, tell her to watch her own safety and report to me what you have done. That is all.'

'I see. And what if I take advantage of my time with May to

persuade her to decline your offer and accept a different one?'

'As I said, we Chinese are great gamblers. I hope that one day she will accept my terms, you hope that somehow a way will be opened for you, that you will at least always stay in her heart. Do you care enough for her to accept my proposition, or is her belief that you do care for her only the illusion of a little trapped bird?'

'Mr Hok, you have certainly laid out your stall well.'

If there was an edge of irony, Mr Hok affected not to hear it. 'So will you buy from my stall, Lieutenant Britton?'

Sandy hesitated. Mr Hok had not made the mistake of appealing to greed by offering money except for the expenses of the trip to Canton. He had not offered anything to him except what he most wanted: a way of having May's company for several days while helping her to escape from her present way of life. During those days together, anything could happen. He preferred to look no further forward than that.

'How far from Canton is this commune you think the most likely target?' he asked.

# 16

The modest and murky office of the South East Asia News and Views Agency was almost deserted. Most of the lights over the word processing screens were already extinguished. Apart from Tom Webster's, only one other light was still burning. Piles of old newspapers and print-outs lay on the shabby brown carpeting. Tom's large glass ashtray was full of half-smoked cigarettes.

From the small window beside Tom's desk, half a dozen floors up, Sandy watched the garish street lighting of the Wanchai district flickering on. Some of the street lights were reflected in the shimmering surface of the harbour and beyond, where modern freighters and traditional Chinese junks mingled at anchor.

'All right,' said Tom Webster, looking up from his word processing screen. 'If you insist, I will give you a definite opinion. Don't touch it with a barge pole. Is that definite enough for you?'

'That's easy for you to say. I could get the time free if I pushed . . . Look, I'm sorry to have bothered you while you're working. I should have phoned first, I shouldn't have just turned up. I'll up anchor and away.'

'Don't be so bloody nautical. Sit down until I've finished this stuff, then I'll buy you a drink at The Mandarin and try to talk some sense into you . . . Janet, love, I've got the present figures for Chinese direct investment in Hong Kong; do you remember the 1985 figure?'

A young Chinese woman sat under the only other light. She

had a small round face and thick spectacles. Janet? Probably her father or mother had been British: in Hong Kong you could never tell what racial mixtures you would encounter.

'Five billion US dollars.'

'Janet, you're a mine of information as per usual. You'll keep things on a straight course here even if I'm ordered out next year.' More quietly he said to Sandy: 'With three million possible applicants for British passports here once the Chinese move in, these are sensitive times, old son. Definitely not the time for freelance experiments in do-goodery, especially if they wear a British uniform.'

'I won't be wearing a uniform and it's not an experiment, it's a serious attempt to reunite the girl with her mother.'

'So Mr Hok says. But do we believe Mr Hok? Janet! What do we know about Mr Hok? Is he still considered honest – I mean as honest as a tycoon like him can be? Bribery of government officials? Involvement with the Triad gangs? Incidents with little girls or little boys?'

'All in personal file under Hok. All there on screen.'

'Okay, Sandy, take that screen beside me, type in the password SMITH and then search for Hok. It won't take me five minutes to finish this piece and by that time you should know more about Mr Hok than I do.'

Tom sounded so patronising that Sandy said: 'Tom, where's that piece you're working on actually going to?'

The answer was a pause and a laugh. 'Ours not to reason why nor where. That is the motto of life on a news agency out here, old chum. Most of our stuff is on offer to all our clients.'

'So it might not actually be published anywhere, ever?'

'Just have a silent look at the Hok file so I can finish this, all right? It's just a straightforward piece of journalism about the present economic position, nothing fancy, nothing cloak and dagger.'

'Who said anything about cloak and dagger?' said Sandy.

The Chinese woman called Janet was looking hard at him over her spectacles. Sandy found the Hok file, which contained the barest information about the companies in which he was interested, and a note that said: 'More on paper, plus pics.'

'Where would paper files and pics be?' enquired Sandy. Without looking away from his screen, Tom said: 'Janet, find what he wants, would you, please?'

She walked over to a large grey cabinet, as big as a wardrobe, in the gloomiest corner of the office. The twin doors were buckled, as if someone in the past had tried to open them with a crowbar. There was a thick polished horizontal steel bar secured across the front of them with two padlocks, one at either end. Janet opened one padlock easily, swung the bar to one side, walked to Sandy's desk and deposited two bulging manila folders on it.

Yellowing newspaper and magazine cuttings offered more information on Mr Hok's business interests. One hinted at a rumour that some of Mr Hok's interests had been given an artificially high value on the market because of share manipulation, not necessarily by him or anyone close to him. That cutting was ten years old and if there had been further developments since, it had gone unrecorded by the correspondents of that vigilant newspaper. It looked as if it had been a quite unsubstantiated rumour. There was nothing else to suggest the slightest breath of scandal, unless a story about large personal bets at Hong Kong's race track was a scandal. But weren't almost all Chinese said to be gamblers and rich ones very heavy gamblers?

Sandy perused the picture file with more interest. There were pictures of Mr Hok making some sort of presentation at the Hong Kong Yacht Club, Mr Hok starting a canoe race for Chinese boys, Mr Hok getting into and out of jet aircraft or helicopters, Mr Hok shaking the hand of three successive Governors, Mr Hok donating a cheque for some kind of medical research and, only a few months ago, when he looked hardly any older than in pictures of him as a much younger man, Mr Hok preparing with other notables to run in a charity race.

'He seems to be Mr Clean,' said Sandy.

'Really? I doubt whether the Archangel Gabriel could survive and prosper in Hong Kong. Anyone in Hok's position would need to know a trick or two.'

'I see, guilty until proved innocent.'

'Come on Sandy, don't be naive. This man will eat you for breakfast. How do you know that what he wants you to do isn't a cover for something else?'

Sandy looked around the office of the South East Asia News and Views Agency, lingering on the padlocks and bar of the filing cabinet. 'Tom, you think everything's a cover for something else. You were born suspicious. Why not start with the proposition that he's just a human being acting from human motives? God knows I've no reason to like the man, but that's what I prefer to believe in this case.'

Tom didn't answer. 'Janet!' he called. 'What bloody year was it that China pulled ahead of the United States as Hong Kong's chief customer?'

'In 1985, January or February. She then had twenty-five point something per cent as compared with the US share of twenty point something per cent.'

'Bloody marvel! There! That wraps it up. Janet, send this stuff out, would you? Sandy, I'm with you.'

In the lift he remarked to Sandy in a less public voice: 'I really would leave it alone, you know, even if you can wangle the leave to do it. Mr Hok would doubtless explain to you the golden rule in Hong Kong, especially at the moment, or anywhere else for that matter. If the possible risk outweighs the possible gain, you leave it well alone.'

'It doesn't outweigh it, not to me.'

'No. Oh well, you'll have to tell your people you're going up to the mainland, you can't just take off like that.'

'I know a travel agency that does four-day visits to Canton. Lots of naval and army chaps go up there on them.'

'Taking Hong Kong Chinese bar girls up there with them?'

'They don't have to know that bit. If she happens to be on the same trip, what's the harm? Apparently a fruit farm near there is one of the sights they show visitors. All we have to do is ask about her mother once we get there. It should all be plain sailing, and with luck – '

'Famous last words. Sandy, old lad. Don't do it. Just don't touch it. Okay?'

They were silent until they were surrounded by the colonial splendours of The Mandarin Hotel, where they seated themselves in deep armchairs in the foyer and Tom ordered scotch-on-the-rocks for both of them.

Sandy knew he must speak his mind before he started drinking or Tom would never take what he said seriously. 'Look, Tom, you knew her before I did. Are you really saying that you personally don't want me to go? Is that what it amounts to? That for your own sake you'd rather keep things as they are? I could understand that.'

Tom Webster took a long sip of his scotch-on-the-rocks. 'No, I'm not saying that, you idiot. I was thinking principally of you.'

'That's nice of you. Then I'm going.'

Tom Webster laughed, took a longer sip and said: 'You were going anyway, weren't you? Quite the Nelson touch all of a sudden. England expects, and all that. Best of luck to you. You may need it.'

# 17

Sam Browne smiled his naughty boy smile as they stood in the vast foyer of the Brotherhood Hotel. Only his deceptive moustache made him look older than Sandy. 'Sure we can go to the city centre ourselves, they got the numbers on the buses in figures like it was London or New York. We could creep out right now.'

'I don't know about that,' said Sandy for the third time.

'Only thing is, we got to remember the place is called Kwang-chow, not Canton any more, or we don't make ourselves very popular, okay?'

'Well – ' said Sandy. May Fong looked from one face to the other as if it were a tennis match. Most of the other faces in the packed foyer were European or American; there were few oriental faces apart from May's.

'Jesus, what is it with you? I can trade ten million Polish whatsits in Hong Kong quicker than I can sell you the idea that we can go it alone. What do you say. May?'

May studied her sandals. 'I leave it to San-di.'

Sam Browne – 'Browne with the final e' he always insisted on being introduced to anyone – was the only member of their tour group who was on his own. Sandy felt this was unfortunate. Sam had attached himself to them from the moment the early morning train pulled into Canton, paying May fulsome compliments and pressing confidences on to Sandy as if they known each other since childhood. It was only the end of the first day in Canton, and already he and May knew that he had been born in New York State; who his father was, what university he himself had attended and that now he was some sort of hot-shot operator in the Hong Kong financial markets and was 'currently without a permanent relationship'. Assimilating all this unsought information had been almost as tiring as the day's official trips to local ceramics factories, conducted by a tall flat-chested Chinese girl with an unsmiling face which suggested her vertically striped blazer and red skirt were worn for the benefit of degenerate but profitable foreigners and that she would have been happier in an unadorned Mao boiler suit of the sort fashionable some years earlier.

Sam could not be escaped. Sandy resented his attentions to May, with whom he of course wanted to be alone, albeit alone in a dragooned group. His moments with her were going to be finite as well as very precious.

'If this fellow is as obtuse in the financial markets as he is in not knowing when he's in the way, he must be millions in debt,' Sandy had whispered as they looked at the umpteenth ceramic Chinese fisherman.

'Please? What is obtuse?'

'Thick.'

'Thick?'

'Oh, never mind.'

If he wasn't careful he would be getting angry with May and alienating her. Ah! Was that what Sam wanted? Did he want her himself? Even more dreadful thought, had he at some time been one of her clients, and were both of them laughing at him behind his back? No. That was the sort of thing that Tom would think. He looked down at May's smiling face and told himself not to be a bloody fool. Sam was just a nuisance who would have to be endured and, as he seemed to know the drill about so many things, used – which served him damn well right.

'Thick?' said May again with a persistent smile.

'Stupid.'

'Ha!' she smiled some more.

It was practically the first time May had smiled since the trip had started. On the train from Hong Kong, she had been visibly ill at ease, tightly clutching her black alligator handbag with the large gilt fastener in the shape of a dragon as if she were frightened a party of Chinese nuns on the other side of the carriage were going to steal it. She had gasped at the sight of the huge Brotherhood Hotel, though she must have been quite familiar with the big hotels in Hong Kong. 'San-di! It looks like prison!' He had had to make a slight fuss, which obviously made her uneasy, to get them rooms on the same floor. At first they wanted her to be in a room two floors above his own, which also made her uneasy. He negotiated a new room for her also on the fourth floor. She protested that the two rooms were not adjoining and he pointed out that they were only four doors apart. For the remainder of the first day she had been restless, possibly because she was in anxious doubt about whether she would find her mother. She took very little interest in the memorial hall to Dr Sun Yat-sen, a blue-roofed pagoda about which their small tourist party raved. 'San-di! They are mostly Americans, yes? And Americans, they are easily impressed.' She dutifully took a trip on a steamer up the Pearl River, which Canton straddled, but showed little animation when he pointed out the workers on the decks of a collier coming in the opposite direction, all wearing big round straw hats and cleaning the decks with primitive brooms. After they left the boat, she gazed aghast at a rack full of bicycles on a main street and commented:

'People do not have cars here. Still they do not have cars.'

'Oh, there are some.'

'As many as London? As many as Hong Kong?'

'Well, no, but – '

'There you are, you see. You are being kind, I think.'

'May, let's not fight.'

She showed little interest in the children who gathered round them every time they stopped – except for one little girl of about seven who wore two long pigtails, a white baggy windcheater, plaid trousers, and scuffed sandals. She patted the child's head. Did the child remind her of what she had been like as a girl before her family had finished up in Hong Kong? They saw troops often, their green uniforms baggy. At every sighting, May held tightly on to his arm, as if they might molest her in some way. What lay behind this fear? Should he ask? He decided it would be better to bide his time.

Inside the department store for foreign buyers near the hotel, she had been openly contemptuous of the thinly-stocked sales floors offering jade souvenirs, wood toys, puritanically-cut clothes, plastic luggage and highly coloured ceramic figures of headsmen with their heavy swords, fishermen with rods and scholars with their books. He bought a fisherman for his father and a scholar for his mother. May declined a silk scarf he offered to buy her. 'In Hong Kong they are much better and much cheaper and you do not have to carry them back,' she said dismissively. 'San-di, do not waste your money.'

He was touched. She herself bought nothing.

Unlike her, he was delighted at everything except the recurrent presence of Sam. It was like having a birthday present (being alone with her) and a Christmas present (seeing a new part of the world) together. He was amused by the solemn party guide's descriptions of factories. He was charmed by the groups of old women they saw frequently sweeping the pot-holed roads with triangular shaped brooms. He was fascinated by the bare-footed Chinese men and women working in the underwater rice fields, walking behind primitive ploughs pulled by water buffalo. He was surprised by the confident, even haughty, air of the young Chinese men high on the iron seats of mechanised ploughs which chugged their way almost as slowly as the water buffalo. May managed only the tiniest of smiles as he pointed these things out to her. No doubt she was embarrassed at the backwardness of her home region of China when compared with her mysteriously adopted Hong Kong.

'This must be old hat to you,' he said more than once.

'Old hat?'

'Sorry. One of my father's favourite expressions. Old fashioned. It's a bit old fashioned itself, perhaps.'

'I see. Yes, old fashioned.'

Sandy was happy not to argue, not to press her in any way; content to let the shared experiences of this trip bind them together. They would have some sort of shared history, however small. He thought almost with pity, when he thought at all, of Mr Hok back in Hong Kong, far away from May and no doubt wondering how the trip was progressing. But Mr Hok had almost entirely slipped his mind by the end of the first full day in Canton, by which time Sandy had learned a little more about her brother, who had apparently been in trouble from the age of twelve and was now undergoing a term in some sort of detention centre for young men. Sandy steered well clear of any mention of a younger sister. He would let her choose her moment for any further revelations in that area, and she had so far shown no signs of broaching the subject. And since Sam had been so obviously cultivating them, she had grown even more reticent.

In the circumstances, thought Sandy, as he stood with May in the foyer of the Brotherhood Hotel, curse this rather pleasant American.

'If you do not want to go on this trip downtown, San-di, we do not go.'

She had agreed to the idea immediately Sam had first suggested it. 'But you want to go.'

'No, not if you do not want to go.'

Sam said pleasantly. 'Come on, May, talk him into it, or we'll leave him to it and do it together. I need someone who can talk Cantonese like a native. You are a native of Canton, aren't you?'

'That would be fun, yes,' said May, dodging the question. She laughed loudly, so that some of the people surrounding them in the vast foyer looked hard at them.

'I'll leave you to talk it over, kiddies,' said Sam and strolled a few paces away to a bookstall.

'All right,' said Sandy hastily. 'Let's go.'

May Fong looked at him keenly. 'We already see the store, San-di. Is very dull in downtown Canton, nothing there for foreigners, nothing as good as in Hong Kong.'

Despite his good resolutions, Sandy's temper snapped. 'Okay, okay, maybe I should go with Sam and leave you here.'

'I come,' said May at once. 'But I think I change clothes, yes?'

'Women!' said Sam, reapproaching as May Fong retreated. 'They have their advantages.'

'Of course, of course, Sandy.'

They did not say much more to one another. It was a long ten minutes before May reappeared, wearing not the white shirt and black silk slacks she had worn all day, but an eye-catching dress in royal blue and gold, with a slit up one side that revealed the outside of almost the whole of one leg. She wore lipstick and eye shadow, too. She carried the same decorated alligator skin handbag. Sandy almost gasped out loud. Paradoxically, the changes made her look even younger and more innocent as well as more obviously beautiful. He wished he could keep all that beauty to himself.

On the way out of the foyer, he could not help saying: 'Is all this for me or him?'

She laughed. 'I do not think he likes me, San-di. A woman

can tell these things.'

'You seem to like him.'

'I think you want me to be nice to him, no?'

'Well, yes, I suppose so, one doesn't want any unpleasantness, it's just that one can have too much of a good thing.'

On the bus, which bore easily understandable figures on the front and back as Sam had predicted, May sat down first and Sam sat beside her. Sandy sat on his own in the seat immediately behind them. At Sam's behest, May enquired in Cantonese what the fares were to the downtown area, and Sam then insisted on paying. 'Any small change, May?' he enquired as the woman conductor approached. 'I only have big notes.'

'No,' said May at once.

Sam looked at her handbag in a way which plainly suggested that she couldn't know for sure unless she looked inside it. It was the sort of over-familiar approach that Sam had adopted from the first. This time it grated on Sandy even more than usual.

'I've some change, Sam. How much is it?'

'Okay, I've just discovered some change in my trouser pocket. I forgot I got some change from that bookstall at the hotel. I'll pay. This is on me.'

Sam spent most of the journey laughing and joking with May. Sandy sat in sullen silence, his attempts to contribute largely obliterated by the engine and road noises from the bus, which was obviously far from new.

After this evening he would run a mile if he saw Sam, and see that May did too. By the time they reached a narrow dimly lit street that appeared to be the terminus, and they got off the bus, followed by a crowd of Chinese, May and Sam appeared to be laughing every other second. Sam had not asked her once about her work, but Sandy expected the question at any second and had resolved to break in with the explanation that she was a secretary. Come to think of it, Sam hadn't asked her questions of any kind, except how long she had been in Hong Kong, and whether she was Cantonese, and she had evaded both. Sandy could not interpret the look that May gave him as they got off the bus and was so irritated that he did not try. The whole evening seemed to be slipping away from him, but he didn't see what he could do about it.

'What now?' he said.

'Up road is street market,' said May. 'Is good for Canton but not so good as Hong Kong.' She sounded bitter. She was quite determined that nothing was going to be as good as Hong Kong. She swept her alligator handbag strap almost aggressively over one shoulder.

May walked between them towards the dim street lights. Sandy put an arm round her waist. He felt her begin to tense, and withdrew the arm. He had agreed not to 'embarrass' her during their trip, charmed by her promise, delivered in a small, little-girl voice, 'Afterwards I make it up to you, San-di.' He had replied: 'I understand.' He wished he could understand now.

As they got close to the lights, Sandy saw the street was lined on both sides with market stalls laden with jackets, trousers, caps, straw hats, bales of cloth, household implements of a type he often didn't recognise, food, bottles of wine and beer, toys and unidentifiable Chinese objets d'art. The street did not have a pavement on either side. On what appeared to be the side of dwellings on each side of the street there were oil lamps suspended on iron hooks. The shadowy illumination made the stall keepers' faces into rather sinister masks.

Groups of Chinese stood idly around some of the stalls, especially those bearing the clothes. They gave the trio keen looks and moved aside to make way for them, their faces bearing the curiosity of people who still saw few Europeans. Or was it that they saw few Chinese girls dressed as May was dressed? In their eyes, the striped or plain jackets and trousers of the Chinese women might have come from a different planet to May's cutaway dress, alligator handbag and restrained but relatively vivid make-up.

'San-di, you see that straw hat with the bird on the side?'

'You want it? I'll get it for you.'

'No, no.'

'Here you are!'

Especially in the dim light, it had been difficult sorting out his notes and coins. He had still pointedly negotiated the deal himself, without reference to either May or Sam.

Sam, paying him attention for the first time since they had left the bus, suddenly said: 'Sandy, why not get something for yourself? Those shirts over there – hundred per cent cotton and very cheap.'

'I'd probably get the wrong size. I don't understand Chinese sizes and neither do you, I imagine.'

'There you're wrong, old buddy. Come on, let's try.'

Sam put a hand into the small of his back to ease him forward towards a stall with a lamp directly above it. It was a simple gesture that might have passed unnoticed from a long-term friend, but the over-fond touch of Sam Browne's hand on his back sent alarm bells ringing through Sandy's mind in a way that he kicked himself for not hearing before. Of course! Even his short time in the navy had given him some discrimination in that respect. Was the ostentatious play for May only window-dressing? If so, it was a relief in one way but certainly not in another. Or was he completely imagining things?

'I think I've got enough shirts, thanks.'

'Oh come on, have you seen the prices? Not a fraction of what you'd pay in London or New York or even in Hong Kong. Here, this one, for instance.'

Sam picked up a red and gilt striped shirt from the stall, checked the size inside the collar, and held it up against Sandy's chest. The group of Chinese around them began to expand into a small crowd. All the Chinese seemed at least a head shorter than themselves. Sandy felt exposed and silly and kicked himself for being civil to Sam Browne in the first place. He could see no sign of May.

He still tried to remain civil. 'I don't think these are the best circumstances for buying shirts, Sam. Where did May get to?'

'Looking at other stalls, I guess. It flatters you, Sandy, it really does. In your currency, about two-pounds-fifty.'

Sandy looked around for May. While he looked, Sam held up another shirt in front of his chest. This one was blue check, with gold piping at the deep collar. 'This would be less adventurous, I guess.'

'I can't see May at all. Have you seen her?'

'Oh, let her be, she's happy enough looking for women's things. Okay, here's another even plainer – '

Sandy half pushed him away as he tried to peer over the top of the crowd that had by now gathered. Little Chinese children were being held aloft by their parents and grandparents to get a better look at the still uncommon occidental visitors in a part of Canton not normally visited by tourists. This helped obstruct the view.

'We've lost her,' he said accusingly.

'Nonsense, Sandy. Okay, if you're not easy in your mind, we'll go look for her . . . Ah! There she is, at the back of the army of admirers, safe as Fort Knox.'

To his relief, Sandy saw this was true. May was watching them both keenly, so keenly that she did not see the young Chinese in the light blue suit come up behind her and grab the strap of her handbag.

'Heh!' shouted Sandy.

Sam Browne acted first. He was already well into the crowd when Sandy began to follow him. Sandy saw the handbag fall to the ground and burst open as the knife wielded by the young Chinese sliced the strap, saw the man reach down for it, saw Sam give him a headlong push that sent him sprawling against one of the least well lit stalls. Sandy plunged towards the stall. He found himself staring at the knife and a pair of granite-like black eyes that left him in no doubt that if necessary the knife would be used. He backed off slowly. He watched the man run into a dark side street, where it would be impossible to find him, especially as no one else in the crowd seemed to be taking a practical interest in the proceedings. Then he turned to see if May was all right.

Sam held her open bag. Wads of Hong Kong dollar notes were on the ground near his feet. He looked into the bag.

With a scream May threw herself at him. She snatched the bag violently out of his hands, closed it and enfolded her arms round it as if it were a baby. The lamplight was dim but not so dim that Sandy failed to see that her eyes were full not of gratitude but of the most piercing hate.

May Fong closed the door of her room when he tried to enter it with her on their return. 'I am tired, San-di. We agree you do not embarrass me here.'

'What's the matter, May? You can tell me. Please tell me.'

'Nothing is the matter. I am tired.'

He wished he had not seen that look of hate in her eyes as she had snatched her handbag back from Sam. Sam was irritating but he had been trying to help. He certainly wished he had not seen that ferocious look.

# 18

There was still no sign of Sam at breakfast.

'May, there must have been some reason you were so angry yesterday. Why don't you trust me?'

'I have told you. He was spying on me.'

'Come on, May, why should he spy on you? It was a natural thing to do, looking at your bag once he'd got it back for you.'

'I do not like him.'

'There was money all over the road. You must have a lot of money with you. Can't you trust me?'

He had vowed to himself that he would not put pressures of any kind on her during this trip. It was to be just a way of getting to know each other: he had not disputed it even when outside her bedroom door last night she had lightly kissed him on the cheek, explained she was tired and upset, and closed the door with him still outside it. Almost immediately the door had opened again and May had said: 'Oh, San-di! I think we are both silly, yes?'

It had been well worth all the irritations and upsets of the day. But she hadn't explained why she had taken such objection to Sam, except for the not very plausible one that he was in some way 'spying' on her.

Every time someone appeared at the top of the entrance steps to the restaurant, Sandy expected it to be Sam. It was always a large Chinese family on their way to fill up one of the huge round tables or middle aged American couples complaining that the weather wasn't as warm as in Hong Kong. The complaint was justified: the single sheet had provided little warmth to Sandy during his sleepless night and

May had said she had forgotten how cold it could be in Canton – it was evidently another of those many things which were 'much better in Hong Kong'.

There were in fact a whole series of interconnected restaurants, linked by archways and passageways, but access to them all was through the one in which they were sitting with a Chinese group. There were only two seats unoccupied at this table, and he had steered May in that direction deliberately so that Sam could not join them even if he did arrive.

'You gave him such a bad time last night he's probably gone back to Hong Kong with his tail between his legs,' guessed Sandy.

'I do not think so. I think last night he may have taken you away so that man could try to take my handbag.'

This was so off-the-wall that Sandy thought it best to ignore it. 'Well, I've seen every other member of our group. Perhaps he can't stand the idea of looking over more factories.'

'I do not like him,' said May again. 'I am glad he is not here.'

She had left the handbag with the sliced shoulder strap in her room and was wearing a black patent leather money belt.

She saw him looking at it. Suddenly she said: 'San-di, I have lost my sunglasses. I must have them.'

'They're probably safe and sound in your room.'

'Of course. On my dressing table.'

'You can collect them before we move off.'

'I shall meet your friend Mr Browne in the corridor, I know I shall. I do not wish that. I do not like him.'

'All right, May, I'll get them for you. If he arrives and sees the empty seat, say I'm sitting here.'

'Yes, San-di.'

The sunglasses were not on her dressing table, a fact Sandy was able to establish only after reassuring the fourth floor's female secret policeman who sat outside the lift, noting all departures and arrivals, that he was not involved in burglary or subversion. Where else would she be likely to leave her sunglasses? He looked around the room without finding what he sought. Her alligator handbag with the severed strap was left on the floor against a leg of the dressing table. He rummaged inside among the lipsticks, nail varnish and such sundry items until his fingers closed over a leather case large enough to hold sunglasses. It did not contain sunglasses, it contained some dog-eared letters addressed to her, bearing postmarks over five years old, and a pristine coloured photograph of a young girl. She was perhaps five years younger than May, but the ivory cheeks, longer and less rounded than the average Chinese, and the large, clear eyes were unmistakable. May's emphatic denials were not, it seemed, correct. May did have a younger sister.

He hardly saw the note-taking dragon by the lift as he returned to the restaurant. He saw almost nothing.

If he asked her about a younger sister she might well just walk out of the restaurant; it was one of her no-go areas. He sat down at the table and tried another question. 'What exactly have you got in that belt, May?'

'You sound strange. Money.'

'Can I ask how much?'

'Not much, San-di. Just a few hundred Hong Kong dollars.'

'May, I find that jolly difficult to believe, or you wouldn't have got in such a state last night when whoever it was snatched it. There was more than a few hundred littered over the road. What is going on? I can't help you if you won't tell me.' Her refusal was a barrier between them, a barrier that last night's brief stay in her room had seemed only at the time to breach.

'All right, San-di. How much do you think it take Mr Hok to buy me out for four whole days?'

The chopstick he had idly picked up snapped in his hand. 'Oh. I didn't think about it.'

'No, San-di. You do not think. Four days at five thousand dollars a day, that is about £2,000 in your currency, I think. Mr Hok give me the money to pay off those who employ me, he tell me to hand over the cash and they will not object to me being away four days, he has arranged it. Twenty thousand dollars, it may seem nothing to you as European, but it is more money than I have ever held in my hand in my life. You know how much workers on fruit communes, vegetable communes, here in Canton are paid?'

'But what's all this got to do with the money in your hand-bag last night?'

'Is same money. Twenty thousand dollars. Mr Hok hand it to me. I do not give it to them.'

Sam had appeared at the top of the restaurant steps, spotting them and moving in their direction at the very moment May sprang this unwelcome news.

'You can't be serious,' said Sandy. 'You are serious! Oh, Christ!'

# 19

The Community Room of the fruit commune was a bleak one. Measuring some fifteen by ten metres, it had plain concrete walls, rectangular gaps where in the West glass windows would have been expected, and two dim, unshaded electric light bulbs hanging from twisted flex. The surrounding fruit trees, within a few metres of the Community Room, prevented much natural light entering.

'What do you use this place for normally?' Sandy had asked their guide when they were directed to the plain wood chairs.

'Entertainment,' the girl in the striped jacket had whispered.

Sandy looked around dubiously. 'What sort of entertainment do the people here get?'

'Please, you ask the chairman.'

It was the answer he had received to several of his questions as they had filed into the room. In front of the lengthwise wall was a long tressle table of unpolished wood. Behind it were a row of plain wood chairs like the ones on which their visiting group was now sitting, shuffling their feet.

Sandy sat with May on his right. On the other side, the middle aged American in the long light brown suede topcoat produced a tiny notebook and a tiny gold pencil and started drawing. His wife, who wore several gold bangles on each wrist and a yellow pyjama suit in silk that might have suited a woman half her age, and who had shown no interest in their tour of the orchards, said: 'Put that away, Douglas. You're not impressing anybody.'

'I want to take notes for the folks back home.'

'They'll care? Who cares? You think this'll mean anything in Pittsburgh?'

Sandy took hold of May's hand and squeezed it. 'Don't worry, May, if your mother's in this commune, we'll find her.'

May had smiled at him briefly before giving his hand a return squeeze. She had been almost completely silent as they had walked around the tight-packed lemon and orange trees.

'Will we have a chance to find Madam Shem?' he had asked their guide.

'You will meet all you want to meet in due time.'

With that they had to be content.

As the members of the party committee which ran the commune filed into the room, he turned to smile reassuringly at May. He had seen her wince. One member of the committee, a young man who looked no more than twenty, had a hump back, a withered arm and a patch over one eye. He slid between the wall and the tressle table to his chair only with the greatest difficulty. No wonder May had winced.

'Poor chap,' said Sandy.

At first May said nothing. Then she said: 'In Hong Kong, they would help him, they have the doctors.'

A middle-aged Chinese woman in the centre of the table banged on it abruptly, and got to her feet. She had a sturdy figure. Her sallow face was long for a Chinese. She was dressed primly in a plain blue jacket and plain lighter blue trousers. Her black-framed spectacles added to her air of severity.

Her voice had the usual guttural Cantonese accent as she spoke hesitatingly in English. 'As chairman of the party committee of this commune, I welcome you. You have honoured us by visiting us from Hong Kong, which will soon be Chinese. First I tell you something about this commune, one of several in this area, which was formed in 1953 as an agricultural producers cooperative of a type pioneered under the wise leadership of Chairman Mao. Within five years, by the time of the Great Leap Forward in 1958, output had more than doubled. For example . . . '

Sandy's attention wandered as the chairman ploughed her way through the impressive tonnages per year of this and that fruit, punctuated by numerous, invariably laudatory, mentions of Chinese politicians. The middle-aged American in the long suede topcoat scribbled away with his tiny pencil but when the chairman finally came to a halt and asked for questions, it was a different American voice which asked the first one, a voice from the back of the room.

'Madam chairman, especially after China assumes responsibility for Hong Kong, would you welcome Hong Kong private investment in your commune?'

Sandy had previously hardly noticed Sam at all. Sam had studiously kept his distance from them, avoiding eye contact even when they were filing around the orchards.

'A question for Beijing, not for me.'

'But madam chairman, you must have considerable influence over such decisions. What would your personal opinion be?'

'It is not for me to have personal opinions. Next question, please.'

Sandy said: 'Could we speak through interpreters to some people on the commune?'

'That may be possible,' said the chairman cautiously.

May squeezed his hand. Sandy assumed it to be a gesture of thanks and went on, 'Why do people decide to come here when I imagine they could make more money in the cities?'

'Decide? It is their duty to be here.'

'You mean they are not here voluntarily? That their freedom is restricted?' Of course! This could be the reason May had not heard from her mother for years.

'In China these things are decided on a rational basis, on where they are of most benefit to the state.'

Sam Browne cut in: 'Will that change when China takes over Hong Kong, or will you still employ only compulsory labour here? If you wish for Hong Kong investment, you will have to convince investors that the labour being used is the most efficient and productive, not merely forced labour.'

'These are questions for Beijing. Next question, please?'

The American in the suede coat asked a question about the suitability of the weather to fruit growing. This produced a relieved answer to which Sandy did not listen. May's fingers were clasped together in her lap so tight that he heard a joint make a cracking sound.

'We'll find her,' he whispered.

May continued to make cracking sounds with her fingers during the answers to a few more questions. The American in the suede coat was about to open his mouth when his wife said, not in a whisper: 'No more questions, Douglas. Who cares?'

'We take up no more of your time,' said the chairman with unexpected decisiveness, got to her feet, picked up a sheaf of papers containing her statistics and began to edge her way out of the room.

The rest happened so quickly that Sandy hardly realised what it was that was happening. May jumped up, pushed her way through the chairs in front of them, reached the front of the table behind which the party committee members were retiring, and started to talk to the chairman. At first the chairman ignored her completely and then waved her away. May took no notice. She followed the woman outside. By the time Sandy had got to the door, and then into the narrow concrete corridor, the commune chairman was disappearing into a doorway, closely followed by May, who slammed the door shut behind them.

As Sandy stood outside the door, wondering what to do next, he saw the rest of the party file out of the building. Except Sam Browne, who appeared to be having quite a bit of trouble tying up a shoelace. He was no more than twenty paces from Sandy, but acted as if he were unaware of Sandy's presence.

Sandy was still waiting outside the door when it opened suddenly. The party chairman glared at him, and shouted to a passing Chinese woman with a shrunken grey face, 'Lai! You come in here!' She spoke in English.

'Yes, Madam Shem.'

Sandy felt as if someone had punched him in the stomach, taking all his breath away. May's mother wasn't some poor faceless worker in this commune, she was the party chairman, the boss. Had it happened since May had last seen her, or had May known it all along?

'And you, come in here!' Madam Shem shouted at him.

With the woman Madam Shem had called Lai, Sandy entered what was obviously the party chairman's office. It was a small square room with the usual concrete walls and a rectangular gap where windows would have been expected. A plain wooden table with two piles of papers, one at either end, was Madam Shem's desk. Between the two piles of papers was an opened envelope and a thick wad of what Sandy recognised as Chinese, not Hong Kong, banknotes.

'You are a witness, Lai! I have refused a bribe offered to me as party chairman by this woman.'

'You don't understand!' screamed May. 'I show you this money to prove I support myself in Hong Kong, your daughter is not a disgrace to you.'

'This woman is no daughter of mine! I have only one daughter in Hong Kong and it is not this woman. I do not acknowledge her. Tell your masters in Hong Kong that they will get no trade concessions from this commune, that I will accept the instructions of Beijing, and I will not be bribed by anyone in Hong Kong.'

Sandy walked forward and held out his arms to May, thinking she might be about to fall. Tears were streaming down her cheeks. He looked at the wad of notes. There was the equivalent of far more than two thousand pounds there: far more than the money she had said Mr Hok had given to her to pass on to her employers and which she hadn't passed on. There must be several times that amount.

'Madam Shem,' he said, 'there must be some mistake . . . '

'A big mistake, yes! You tell your friends that I am not for sale to corrupt persons in Hong Kong or Europe, that the money this woman tried to force on me is all there, returned to you. Count it.'

May picked up the money.

'That is right,' said Madam Shem. 'You degraded plaything of the capitalists, you disgrace to the Chinese nation that bore you! You are no daughter of mine! Go back to where you come from in Hong Kong and sell yourself to rich capitalists. That is all you are good for!'

Sandy tightened his grip on May's shaking shoulders. 'Madam Shem, May came here to find you. That is the reason she came here.'

Madam Shem's eyes behind her thick spectacle lenses were even more like stone. 'If you believe that, you are a bigger fool than she is. Lai, you are a witness to all this. Take your money back to your friends in Hong Kong. This incident will be reported. This is a delicate time as you know, otherwise I would have the militia arrest you immediately for currency offences.'

Sandy said: 'Madam Shem, I know nothing about any currency offences and I doubt whether May does either.'

'You poor stupid European, you know nothing about anything.'

'I know that May's had a hard life and that it's all too easy to judge her.'

Madam Shem walked over to the door and threw it open. Sam Browne was standing almost directly outside it. 'You leave now, please,' she said in the same flat, hard voice. 'Go back to your sty in the West where you will feel most at home and take this woman with you. She is yours, not mine.'

Sandy knew it was best to say nothing at all. He said: 'May wanted to come because she missed her mother. If mothers behave to their children here as you have done to May, Madam Shem, perhaps there are worse sties here than in the West. Come along, May.'

He kept one arm round her shaking body as she made her tearful way out of the office, out of the building and straight into the tour bus. He was shaking, too. He remained there with her, not saying much, until the rest of the party boarded the bus, ready to leave. It could not have been much more than ten minutes. It seemed a very long time indeed. Only when the rest of the party climbed aboard did she immediately stop weeping and force a smile.

'What a beastly thing, May. I really am overcome with admiration for you, you know, as well as sympathy.'

Sam Browne sat immediately behind them on the journey back to the hotel. He did not speak once.

# 20

The train was slow. It was still too fast for Sandy: it was bearing him towards Hong Kong and away from her.

She sat in the seat facing him, looking in the direction of Hong Kong. She had pointedly taken that seat the moment she had set foot on the train. He saw her unsmiling ivory face and the flooded rice fields of the Republic of China as they slowly moved away from him, into his past. He had a leaden feeling that she might be moving into his past, too.

For a long time, as he watched the workers in the rice fields watching the passing train without abandoning their stooping position, merely turning their lowered heads, he hadn't trusted himself to speak.

'Despite everything, May, I wouldn't have missed the last four days for anything. I mean being with you. Last night was – '

She leaned forward and put a hand over his mouth. 'San-di! That was private.'

'It was the happiest night of my life, May Fong, even better than that first time.'

The American woman sitting on the other side of the coach, who had yesterday worn the yellow pyjama suit, today wore a black pyjama suit which suited her no better. She turned to her husband and said something Sandy didn't catch. May must have heard, however, because she pressed herself back in her seat and started fiddling with her alligator handbag. The strap was still sliced.

'Dolores, suppose we mind our own goddam business? That's what I'm telling you.'

'Who cares what you're telling anybody? Who cares?'

Sandy could now guess what she must have said in the first place. He put a hand on May's knee and said: 'I don't regret anything! May, I really don't. Not even when you've been . . . well, pretty bad-tempered with me. There's something hanging over you, isn't there? What is it? Why won't you tell me?'

May, who had previously displayed no interest in the passing rice fields, had turned her head away and now appeared to be transfixed by them.

'San-di, we talk about something else, please.'

'We seem to be running out of subjects we can discuss, don't we? Maybe we could talk about why it is that all the best Americans seem to stay at home? Okay, so you're not in the mood for jokes. What do you think those people out there in the fields are thinking, May? Are they wishing the train could magically scoop them up and bear them away to Hong Hong and other exciting places? Or are they resenting the intrusion of foreign faces and foreign wealth, and wishing they'd go away?'

'San-di, you speak strange things again. I do not resent your wealth.'

'I was speaking generally. In any case, I don't imagine any-one could think me seriously wealthy – not compared with Mr Hok, for instance.'

She fell silent so long that he thought she was going to remain silent for ever. When she spoke she did not mention Mr Hok. 'You are wealthy compared with me when I was girl. You know nothing of how we had to live then. Oh, San-di, I do not blame you. You should have nothing more to do with me, I think.'

'I don't know whether I could manage that, May. I really am sorry about what happened with your mother.'

'It would have been better if you had not spoken, San-di. Yes, I know you meant good, you always mean good but – '

'I know. I'm sorry, May, I thought your mother was a hard woman, not at all like you, and that's the truth of it.'

When she gave him a look he didn't like at all, he added quickly: 'But I suppose you took her by surprise, and she may be having second thoughts by now, sending you away like that. Perhaps she'll try to find you when she's calmed down.'

'She does not know where I am in Hong Kong.'

'She does now. I gave one of the officials the address of the Hot Cat Club and asked him to pass it on when she'd calmed down.'

'You did that? You gave her my address?'

They were passing through what had been the Lowu Main Gate, where Chinese trains had once had to stop for passengers to change to Hong Kong trains for the rest of the journey. Now trains from either side went straight through.

'I thought I should. You were so upset, you wouldn't have thought of it.'

On the platform they were passing without stopping was a group of army soldiers, their green suits baggy, their rifles over their shoulders.

'May, you'll feel better when we're back in Hong Kong. You love Hong Kong, don't you? Everything was always better in Kong, wasn't it – all the time we were in Canton you were thinking that? Suppose I were to pack in the navy, and get some sort of job in Hong Kong?'

'You are laughing at me, San-di. You ask me to trust you, but you laugh at me.'

'May, we'll soon be there. We must talk. What was the money you offered to Madam Shem?'

'I offer her money to show I can keep myself in Hong Kong, so my mother think well of me.'

'No, May, you had that money in your money belt, sure, but you also had that envelope you tried to give your mother.'

'A letter.'

'No, May, not a letter. Was it money from Mr Hok, was that it? Does Mr Hok have business connections with your mother? Does Mr Hok want to have business connections with the commune when China takes over Hong Kong? Does he want to reunite her with her daughter and send her money at the same time? Is that it? I used to be a journalist, you know. Not for long, but I was one once. I've been trying to think like Tom Webster would think. Why can't you trust me, May? Look, we'll be in the station at any moment. We're through the New Territories, we're into Kowloon. Once we're into Hong Kong Island . . . I'm just frightened of losing you forever, May, do you believe me? What was the money in the envelope?'

'Was no money in envelope.'

'May, I can't believe that. I'd like to believe you, but I can't. Tom thought I shouldn't have come on this trip, but I'm glad I did, I shall always be glad that I was alone with you for four whole days.'

'With me and your friend Sam Browne.'

'He's not my friend. I'm bloody glad we've seen less of him. May, what was in the envelope?'

He was still asking her that question as the train pulled into the station.

'And you leave that woman my address!' she said as she carried her suitcase and her handbag off the train, despite his offers of help. Once off the train, she wheeled her suitcase as if he were not there.

'May, we must talk about this! We must talk!'

'Nothing to talk about. You let go my arm, please!'

The station concourse was vast, more like an airport than a railway station. Crowds of people were milling around, but May marched ahead like an unstoppable army.

'May, I meant what I said about leaving the navy.' He kept

a tight grip on her arm, not caring about what others around them, including the other members of their tour group, thought.

'You take your hands off me, please.'

'Please calm down, May. You're getting hysterical. Things may not be as bad as you think, you know.'

'You stupid Englishman!' she said without stopping. 'I try to stay in China! I think I take money for Madam Cat and money for Madam Shem and stay in China! I think I just show it to my mother and keep it!'

'May, you don't know what you're saying. That doesn't make any sense.'

'You think in your stupid, ignorant European way you can change people's lives, you can do great miracles, you can – '

'May! Everything I've done, I've done because I love you. I love you! You must believe that, or nothing makes any sense, nothing at all. I think you love me, too. Don't you? Stop all this. I love you.'

She turned to look at him and he would never forget the look on her face. 'You use words that are stupid. You speak stupid things. You take your hands from me, please, or I call police and make things bad for you.'

His angry reaction was to tug at her so hard that she had to turn and face him. 'I don't think anyone's going to call the police. Look, May, let's find a bar and talk about this. You owe me that.'

'I owe you nothing.' She shrieked out something else in Cantonese which he didn't understand. He did not release his grip on her arms. He began pulling and pushing her towards the station exit. She screamed again in Cantonese. Chinese and Europeans looked at them both with disapproval. Whether Sam Browne, who was also making for the exit, saw them or not Sandy wasn't sure.

One thing of which he was immediately sure was the identity of the two British sailors directly ahead of them.

'Good afternoon, sir!' said Ferguson, looking at them both with the suggestion of a smile on his sallow face. 'Nice weather we're having.'

Simons unconvincingly pretended not to see him.

Why was it that, like a magnet, you always attracted the people you least liked to see at the time when you least liked to see them? Sod's law? On the other hand, if anyone were interested, it would have been quite easy to find out the arrival time of the train on which the tour group was returning.

Sandy ran after May, who turned when almost at the exit and slapped him hard across the face. He tried to get hold of both her arms. She brought one high-heeled shoe down hard on his instep. He shouted with pain, but did not let go. She lashed out at his eyes with her nails. That made him let go. She flew out of the exit and into a cab before he could get both eyes open again.

Ferguson and Simons were standing nearby, even Simons no longer pretending not to see him.

# 21

'Yes, Britton, but any sort of trouble with the Chinese just now would be highly inconvenient, do you see? The Governor would hate it. That absolutely mustn't happen.'

Captain Wembley's room was large by naval standards, but small enough for the cigar smoke to be stiflingly thick. Sandy tried hard not to cough. He was in enough trouble already.

Captain Wembley was a large man who smiled from long force of habit. He intended one day to drive one of the Royal Navy's remaining large carriers. He was sure that not being a shit got you further than being a shit, and so far he had been proved right. You only kicked people when you had to and then, by god, you let everyone know you had done it. He was popular with both officers and men, though he took care not to be too popular. On his walls were some of the oils he painted while ashore, on his shelves a few of the historical novels he read while afloat and many silver sporting trophies. There was a chintz-covered bunk and chintz curtains. On a black pad-locked filing cabinet stood a brass tray bearing whisky and sherry decanters, a bottle of gin and three glasses. His desk was empty except for a silver cigar box. He opened it.

'Sure you won't, Lieutenant? This is all quite unofficial. Not the best news, of course, to get when I return from seeing our friends in Singapore.'

'Quite sure, thank you, sir, I don't smoke.'

'Just as well to have at least one vice one doesn't pursue.' He relit his cigar with a monogrammed silver lighter. Captain Wembley's voice had only the slightest edge. 'Personal, you say?'

'That's right, sir. And I never hit her, whatever the caller may have said.'

'Anonymous telephone call for the Captain, pretending not to know the Captain's name. Bit overdone – almost certainly someone from the ship. Bad business. Any idea who?'

'Ferguson or Simons, sir. I saw them at the station yesterday when we arrived back.'

'Ah! The fellows involved in that damn silly bike business. That would figure. Any evidence?'

'Not without having heard the voice of the caller, sir.'

'How could you have heard the voice of the caller? Provided I am satisfied with your answers, there was no call. Understood? The trouble is, Lieutenant, that nothing in Hong Kong at this present time can be completely "personal", certainly nothing touching the dignity of an officer of the Royal Navy. One must never overlook that fact. Gossip within the confines of the wardroom is one thing, anonymous telephone calls from public call boxes about the behaviour of officers towards Chinese people in public places is quite another – especially when the non-existent informants say the Chinese person involved was a bar girl who was returning by train to Hong Kong with you.'

'I informed the First Lieutenant I was going on the trip to China, sir, it being my leave, and there was no objection.'

'You forgot to mention, however, that you were not going alone, that you were going with a lady whose occupation is, shall we say, nebulous and whose own behaviour in public seems to be equally nebulous. Are those scratches still painful?'

'She's been under great strain, sir, and that was partly my fault.'

'Yes? You can speak freely. We are not on the record.'

'Sir, the girl does work as a bar girl. She hasn't been doing it for long. A lot of girls here are driven to it, sir. It's different over here – it's not like being a tart in Soho or something like that. She needs money to support relatives. Since she left her mother in China, she's been a sort of mother to the rest of the family here in Hong Kong. I took her up to Canton, sir, in the hope of reuniting her with her mother, acting on some information I had been given. It was a disaster, for which I blame myself. That's the truth, sir, whatever Ferguson or Simons may have said.' He had not, and would not, mention Mr Hok.

'You mean whatever the unknown caller may have said. We have no definite proof it was a naval person.'

'Quite so, sir. She took it hard, sir, when her mother refused to speak to her, didn't want to know her. She appears to be a highly placed official in the Communist Party there, sir. Not what you'd call the motherly type. A rather hard lady.' He had not and would not mention the money.

'A "hard" lady who disapproves of what her daughter's doing, perhaps?'

'Yes, sir, but there are ways of saying things. To reject your own daughter – '

'We must leave the Chinese to sort out their own affairs, don't you think? Whatever you may think or I may think isn't going to make tuppence worth of difference a year from now. Our job, Britton, is to reinforce Britain's naval presence wherever our political masters decide that may be necessary, not to concern ourselves with the past, however glorious that past. We can't rewrite or wipe out history.'

'The trouble is, sir, that Miss Fong is to do with my present, not my past. My feelings for her are unchanged. I love her, sir.'

Captain Wembley looked unblinkingly at Sandy for an eternity. 'Oh,' he said at last. 'I see. Oh dear.'

'And I'm thinking of checking out of the navy, sir, and coming back to Hong Kong.'

This time Captain Wembley did not hesitate. 'That sounds like a thoroughly bad idea. My dear fellow, the only way you could do that would be to be dishonourably discharged, and I don't think any of us would fancy that. Think of the ship if not of yourself.'

'I could buy myself out. She wants to go to university here, sir. She helps to support her brother, who's some sort of tear-away who's always been in trouble with the Hong Kong authorities, and is now in some sort of detention centre.'

'Charming mother-in-law, charming brother-in-law.'

'She can't help them being related, sir.'

'True. Look here, Lieutenant, consider that your last statement to me was never made. Understood? Forget it and forget her and her family. All this sort of thing's not very good for a sailor's career, you know. Or his life, for that matter. Where can it lead, except to disappointment and grief on one side or both? On Monday – three days time – we put to sea again. We may be back here in the foreseeable future, we may not.'

It was the first time that Sandy had heard the ship was leaving in three days. 'Three days, did you say, sir? Is that all?'

'The electronics should be sorted out by then, and we'll be off. It should be posted around the ship in the next half hour. Now I can't officially ask you not to see this lady again – '

'Perhaps you should, sir.' Sandy felt utterly weary and empty. 'Perhaps it would make things easier in a way. I keep thinking about her, you see. Last night I kept seeing her face all the time and wondering where she was and what she was doing. I've never felt anything like it before. It's not what you think, sir – '

'How do you know what I think? All I can do is tell you quite candidly to behave in public and in private at all times in a way suitable to the dignity of an officer of the Royal Navy. As far as the lady in question is concerned, I have no intention of making things easy for you in any way whatsoever, certainly not by issuing any orders about who you should meet and who you shouldn't. I'm not a bloody nanny. Just think carefully about the lady, Lieutenant. Think of her in the kindest way possible, by all means, but don't get yourself involved in anything that can damage the reputation of the Royal Navy and your own life. Is that fair?'

'Very fair, sir. If I were to see her just to say goodbye – '

'Don't tell me anything I haven't asked you to tell me, Lieutenant. *War Lion* is a first class ship with first class officers and men who know their way around, are we agreed on that?'

'Of course, sir.'

'Excellent. I'm glad we had this little talk, Britton. I'm sure all this will soon be behind you, and that you'll go far in the Royal Navy. Enjoy your remaining days here.'

As he walked out, Sandy wondered how he was to keep her out of his mind for seventy-two hours. Perhaps he could manage it if he never saw her again. Perhaps he could manage it if he never saw Tom again – Tom was bound to mention her name. Perhaps if he never spoke her name out loud again the pain in his nerve endings would one day go away?

Rubbish. Of course the pain wouldn't go away. Despite what the Captain had said, it was still more likely that he would somehow find her and leave the navy.

# 22

'Tom, is May there?'

Too long a pause. Then Tom Webster said: 'She came at eight, as usual. That's all that was usual about it, as a matter of fact. Where are you?'

'Telephone box near the harbour. They said she hadn't been back to the Hot Cat. Is she still there? Is she all right?'

By eleven that night he knew he would have to ring Tom's number again or go back to the ship. He could not face the sort of unthinking good-natured banter he would have to face if he went back aboard while still on leave. 'Back already? Not as hot as you'd thought, eh? Dear, dear, poor Sandy!' Just the sort of thing they said in the wardroom. Normally merely irritating. Intolerable now.

He had rung Tom's number three times already, as he walked round and round Wanchai, and had got the answering machine each time. That told him nothing: Tom could be there, and so could May, both too busy to answer the phone. Alone in those unfamiliar telephone kiosks, in an area he didn't know well, especially after dark, he had felt more lonely than he had ever felt in his life.

'She's all right. What about you? I gather you had some difficulties.'

'That's one way of putting it. We had one hell of a row on the railway station just after we'd got back, and she ran off. It was a washout. Her mother went off the deep end as if some-one was trying to bribe her.'

'And were they, do you think?'

'I don't know what to think. She was even talking about

staying in China. I don't think she knows what she wants. What time did she get to you? She must hate me a lot, she thinks I was the one who brought all this on her.'

'Early. Were your ears burning? They should have been. She gave me an inventory of your sins and omissions that lasted half an hour and then gave a repeat performance with slightly more emphasis. I couldn't get a word or anything else in.'

'Is she still there?'

'Love-hate rather than hate, I'd say, wouldn't you? It got a bit wearing, to be absolutely frank. At one point I lost my cool and told her she seemed more interested in rubbishing you than in pleasing me. And that's virtually all that happened Chez Webster this fine night, if that gives you any satisfaction.'

Sandy fished in his pocket for some more change. 'Did you say she was still there?'

'I didn't blame her for wanting to leave early. She seems to be distinctly off Europeans, though in one case I rather take leave to doubt that it runs very deep. Did you see what was in the envelope she tried to show or pass to her mother?'

'No, I hoped you might know.'

'Look, Sandy, calm down. I phoned Mr Hok two hours ago.'

'Janet, that girl in the office, said you weren't there.'

'I phoned him from here. I'm seeing him tomorrow morning to discuss business and other matters.'

'How did you manage that? Tomorrow's Saturday.'

'This is Hong Kong, not dozy London. I was able to make him see the advisability of seeing me. The money she took that she should have handed over to her employers from Hok when he bought her out for four days, is virtually intact, except for her taxi ride here, which I've given her. We'll get that to her employers as soon as we can. When I know more from Hok about what the other money was for, maybe we can return it to him and he'll let bygones be bygones. I'll let you know. Can I ring you on the ship?'

'Better not, I'll get in touch with you. Tom, I've asked you twice if she's still there, and each time you've given me a diplomatic answer that I should take to mean no, but you haven't actually said no. You see? Even May said at one point that I'm starting to think like you. Well?'

'Sandy, dear old chum, don't you think you've become more than a little paranoid where May is concerned?'

'You see? You've done it again. Look, my money's running out and I haven't got any more. She can't have any money if she had to use some from that twenty thousand Hok handed to her to pass over.'

'Dear Sandy, your ship sails on Monday. Don't you think it would be best for all concerned if you went back to the ship, stayed there safely until you sail on Monday, and tried to forget her?'

'Tom, if she's not there, where do you think she is?'

'Not at a convent taking holy vows, you can be fairly sure. My dear old chum, she has more than one client, had you thought of that?'

'There you go again! I think she's still there. I'm coming over.'

'Sandy, coming here's not a very good idea at all. No. Keep calm. After I've seen Hok tomorrow . . .'

Sandy said stubbornly: 'I'm coming over.'

The line went dead.

Tom Webster said, 'Shit!' and put the phone down. He was dressed only a pair of salmon pink yachting trousers. It was hot in the Kennedy Road apartment, and to him it felt hotter than it was.

May Fong, who had been watching him carefully throughout the conversation, was dressed in the same clothes she had worn

152

for the return journey from Canton. It was easy to see they had not been disturbed. She said: 'I go now!'

'No, I think you'd better stay, he's got to come of age at some time.'

'No! I go!'

'May, don't be a fool. Where will you go? You can't go anywhere until your people have got their money back.'

'It does not matter.'

'Of course it matters. It matters to that young twit and it matters to me.'

'That is nice of you to say, but I go now!'

'May, Sandy won't eat you.'

'Perhaps I eat him.'

'He wouldn't be very tasty . . . Oh, for god's sake, May. . . . '

She was half way to the door when he came up behind her and put his arms round her, clasping her hands to prevent her escaping. She brought her heel down the front of his shin and trod hard on his instep. He let go. She had her hand on the door knob when he grabbed her again.

'Please! You let me go!'

He held her in a steely grip and swung her round to face him. His patience snapped. 'Bloody bad value tonight, May Fong!' He manhandled her closer, pressing her to him. She struggled furiously, stumbled when one high heeled shoe twisted under her and fruitlessly tried to claw his face.

He hit her round the side of the head with the flat of his hand, hard. He said immediately, dropping his arms to his sides, 'I'm sorry, May. I mean that, I'm very sorry indeed. I shouldn't have done that.'

Incredibly, she merely smiled. He had never previously believed that orientals were any more inscrutable than anyone else. Then she opened the door and made for the lift. He did not try to stop her.

# Part Four

# 23

1841

Charlie Webster and Billy Britton walked the narrow, muddy tracks and passageways of Hong Kong near the harbour, periodically breaking out into loud laughter. They had already consumed many rums that day, each assuring the other with mock solemnity that it was only to kill the bugs so that with luck they might live to see 1842 and beyond. What they saw in the streets did not worry them: neither man related other people's suffering to himself. Both men were solely preoccupied with their own problems.

'Not able to set foot inside my own room!' guffawed Charlie Webster.

'Hardly dare go back to the ship!' roared Britton.

As they made their way through the packed rows of wooden huts occupied by the Chinese, laughing immoderately at the blank, uncomprehending yellow faces of the women as they squatted in the narrow doorways, often with sleeping or screaming children in their laps, Charlie Webster put an arm around his friend's shoulder.

Billy Britton shook it off. He had not had so much rum that he was prepared to let discipline slip too far on what passed for a public street, where they might at least in theory meet a senior officer at any moment, though what a senior officer would be doing in such a godforsaken hole he could not begin to guess.

Webster dismissed the rebuff with a laugh. In his present mood he would have laughed at anything. 'Irritable, are we,

Billy? Suffering from love? You must admit it's a great compliment she's paid you. You must have made a great impression on her, to put it politely, to persuade her to follow you around like this. Like a devoted dog. What did you do to her, and would it make me blush?'

'Better if I'd made no impression at all, Charlie. I told you it was a mistake to see her again. This is the third day she's been hanging around the ship, asking for me.'

' "Fat officer with golden head." I thought that rather good. Anyone who's not got a waist you can put your fingers round is a fatty to these people. Don't be too hard on yourself. What else is there to do in this godforsaken hole except see people like her again? And again?'

'All the same, I feel like a man who's picked up a stray dog.'

'Bitch.'

'Bitch. You can say that again. A bitch nuisance.'

'You won't shake yourself free now, Billy, mark my words. There's something about you she likes, yes, indeed; and now she's had it three times, you can't blame her for not wanting to give it up, whatever it is. She can't forget you, Billy.'

Billy Britton suddenly turned sullen. 'Oh do jack it in, Charlie. I'd damn well like to forget her, that's a fact. Nobody takes any notice of her, thank the Lord, but you can see it could get nasty if they could make head or tail of what she's saying in her heathen lingo.'

'Confess it, Billy, you rather like the conquest you've made.'

'Oh, she was all right on her back, Charlie, I don't deny that. But why do women have to spoil it all by hanging around afterwards? Especially women like her? I can never work it out.'

'You're an officer, old man. Smart uniform and all that. Marvellous catch for a girl like her, if she thinks she really has caught you.'

'I swear if she shows up at the gangplank again, I'll . . .

I'll . . . I don't know what I shall do. An officer can't thrash even a native in public. Did you know that? You must admit it's pretty thick. It's bloody persecution. A good thrashing might cure her.'

'What about my feelings? What about when she turned up at my humble abode and let everyone know she was after you, not me? Humiliating, Billy, damned humiliating, you must admit that.'

'Bit of a bloody relief, too, I shouldn't wonder?'

'Just a bit!'

Both men dissolved into more peals of laughter. Billy had already forgotten his pique. The women and the old men stared at them from the dark doorways of their hovels. Charlie Webster drew a pewter flask from his rumpled white jacket. But Billy Britton drew the line at drinking in the street in front of witnesses – even in the sewer these chinks called home. He waved the flask aside. If he drank, it would be in the discreet safety of the ship or of Charlie's quarters; or at least in a quite empty street. He wanted to be made up to Admiral before he was finished with the navy. Though he valued his pleasures, he had no intention of finishing up like a version of Charlie Webster, who could afford to indulge himself in practically any way he choose precisely because his career was not going to progress much further, if at all. Billy did not tell his friend this. Of course the man was his friend, but one did not play with a completely visible hand of cards with anybody, even one's friends. Not if one were wise, as he intended to be where it counted.

They wandered back towards the temporary colonial service compound, relieved to get away from the stinks of the heathens who were now going to be an eternal part of the good old empire.

Outside the gates of the compound they saw the all-too-familiar figure of May Fong. She was arguing and gesticulating at the soldier on the gate, who was desperately trying to keep his rifle at the correct angle while thrusting her away from him every time she lunged at him.

'Oh dear! To the ship instead, I think, Charlie! Unless you'd care to take her off my hands.'

'I think not, in the circumstances. The ship it is, if that's all right.'

'A few drops of grog aboard will do us the world of good. Better than hanging around here until she sees us. Come on.'

The two men did not, however, proceed straight back to *War Lion*. Billy suddenly remembered he would have to take back some chink gift for his mother. They searched some of the crude stalls set up between the colonial compound and the harbour. It was some time before they were in sight of the ship, Billy clutching his heavy jade fruit bowl.

Both men came to a sudden halt.

'Damn!' said Billy Britton. 'Damn and blast. What insolence!'

'Unbelievable!' agreed Charlie Webster.

May Fong was at the gangplank of the ship, this time arguing with a seaman at the near end of it. There was no sign of the official watch at the head of the gangplank.

The rum they had consumed earlier was now beginning to congeal the contents of their sour stomachs and to tell on their tempers, especially Billy Britton's. 'To hell with her!' he grunted. He walked straight towards the gangplank as if she were not there.

'Bill-li, Bill-li, I worship you, you want me? I come to you, Bill-li!'

Charlie Webster failed to stifle a guffaw. 'Thinks you're a god, Billy. I warrant she'd give it you for free.'

'Yes, yes, free! Free!'

In her eagerness to get at him, May Fong's silk blouse started to slip off one shoulder and one small foot slid put of her sandals. She clutched his arm. The fruit bowl slipped from Billy's grasp, and smashed on the ground.

'Damn you!' he shouted. He pushed her violently.

She stumbled backwards and fell. Almost instantly she was on her feet again, grabbing for him as he made his way rapidly up the gangplank, cursing and shouting. 'Watch! Watch! Where the hell's the watch? I'll skin someone alive for this!'

A frightened-looking young seaman suddenly appeared, looking flustered. Britton glared at him. 'Where were you, man? Get rid of this crazy woman, you hear? Get rid of her! I don't care how you do it, just do it.'

'Aye, aye, sir!'

First the young seaman go hold of her by the shoulder. She shook him off. He grabbed her by the hair. She screamed and kicked his shin. He let out a bellow of pain and struck at her with his fist. He missed.

Charlie Webster let out an hysterical giggle as May Fong and the young seaman swayed on the gangplank. The giggle erupted into explosive laughter when the seaman pushed May Fong away from him so violently that she swayed, desperately tried to find the gangplank rope with one hand and just managed to hold on.

On the deck of *War Lion*, just by the gangplank, Billy saw a pail of filthy water which had obviously been used for swabbing decks. He grabbed it and, as May Fong gained her balance and came towards him again, let her have the contents straight in the face. As she staggered backwards, soaking wet, he shouted to no one in particular, 'Get this mad woman off the ship!' He turned his back and set off for his cabin, Charlie Webster wheezing and stumbling with laughter close behind him.

Afterwards the only thing that made Billy Britton slightly

uneasy was the fact that the man who gave May Fong his arm and helped her down the gangplank was Ferguson. He didn't know why this made him uneasy because, whatever he thought, Ferguson, or any other riff-raff from the lower decks, were in no position to do him any harm. After he and Charlie Webster had taken some more grog, he thought no more about it.

# 24

1841

May Fong's brother Lee-yen took her by the shoulders and shook her until her soaked silk blouse fell open. This angered Lee-yen even more. He slapped her across the face with the flat of his hand, abusing her in guttural Cantonese.

'Ha! Whore! Disgrace to our mother! Plaything of the invaders! Animal!'

Lee-yen was younger than May Fong, a small slender youth with a round intense face and large piercing black eyes. He considered himself a man, and it was the business of a man to protect his sister, even if she were older than he. He was the man of the house, even if the house consisted of no more than a rough structure of wood a quarter of a mile from the waterfront, a hovel only just large enough to hold Lee-yen, May and their father and mother.

The father said nothing, either against May or in her defence. He lay on the dirt floor at the very furthest corner of the shanty, gently puffing on his pipe of opium.

The sight of his father added to Lee-yen's rage. 'Plaything of heathen sailors! Have I not told you before? I would rather see you dead than the whore of the invaders. Look at me!' He struck May Fong across the face again and then, suddenly losing all restraint, pounded at her face with his fists. Their mother forced herself between them. The father did nothing except puff away on his opium pipe.

'Do not talk like this, my son. It is dangerous to say these things about the British. The British bring many benefits, they bring us work – '

'Work? The work of dogs.'

Lee-yen pointed at his father. 'Do they bring him work? Would he be able to do it even if they brought it, thanks to the other things they bring? One day before long we will throw them out. Let them declare this a British colony. Let them! One day it will be ours again, and we will have no more opium brought here from India and other places in their heathen empire! One day – '

'My son, you are sick in the head, you should watch your words. The British are here with the agreement of the Emperor – '

'Agreement at the end of a gun!'

'By agreement. How many times must I tell you? You will finish in their prison if you talk like you talk. You will break your mother's heart and surrender yourself to evil spirits. The gods say – '

'I do not believe in spirits, mother. I do not see spirits. All I see is a whore going with sailors – '

'He is not a sailor!' screamed May Fong, trying to shake herself free of his grasp. 'He is an officer. You hear me, an officer! He has money. He has high position in England. He told me he would take me there – '

'Fool! He would tell you anything.'

'What I tell you is true. He is an officer. I know that by his uniform. And he was on the ship with Mr Webster of the colonial service, which a common sailor would not be.'

Lee-yen slapped her across the face again. 'Ha! Mr Webster! Another of your clients, yes?'

'I tell you Billy is an officer. He did not mean to have me thrown off the ship. He did not mean that I should fall in the harbour. It was an accident, a mistake. I think he was trying to save me.'

Lee-yen took her by the shoulders and shook her. 'Gullible

fool! You make yourself ridiculous because of this man. He may wear a better uniform, yes, he may do that, but he is a sailor like the rest of them.'

'He told me he would take me to England. I try to remind him of this – '

'Take you to England? He was making a fool of you. Yes! If I thought he really wanted to take you from us, I would kill him!'

Lee-yen reached into the pocket of his cotton jacket and produced a slender knife not more than four inches long. 'I would kill him with this, you believe me? I kill him if he ever touches you again!'

The father, looking like a very old man, though he was scarcely more than forty years old, lay quietly on the floor, smoking his pipe and saying nothing.

It was the mother who tried again to restrain Lee-yen. 'You talk wildly, my son. You should ask forgiveness of Kuan Yin, the goddess of mercy, she who looks down and hears the cries of the world. Let her bring you comfort. We cannot meddle in matters concerning the British. It is dangerous. If the Emperor has granted Hong Kong to the British, he had his good reasons.'

'The Emperor! That degenerate!' Lee-yen looked wildly around him as if the small size of the hut was physically choking him. Finally he pushed May Fong away from him with a gesture of disgust and rushed from the hut, cursing and screaming. He still held the knife.

The mother put her arms round her daughter in the hope of comforting her.

'Mother, will Lee-yen hurt him?'

'He will be back, my daughter. He is full of male rage and fire at this moment, but before long he will think better of it and return.'

'No! He will hurt him. He will ruin everything! Billy said he would take me to England!'

'You must not believe such things, child. It will never be.'

May Fong pushed her mother aside. 'He will hurt him!' Still in her wet silk blouse, she ran out into the narrow alleyways, looking left and right for her brother. He was out of sight. She sped swiftly back towards the harbour. The father stayed where he was, silently smoking his pipe of opium.

When she got within sight of HMS *War Lion*, May Fong saw her brother walk to the foot of the gangplank, ignoring shouts from a group of seaman on the quay for him to stop. She paused, gasping for breath. She saw Lee-yen start to mount the gangplank. She saw Billy Britton appear at the head of the gangplank. She shouted out his name. She wanted to warn him, but he took no notice of her shout, concentrating on her brother as he mounted the gangplank and began to walk towards him.

May Fong was already at the foot of the gangplank, screaming for Lee-yen to stop, when her brother suddenly lunged at Billy Britton with the knife. Britton quickly jerked to one side. He took the knife in the arm instead of in the stomach.

May Fong screamed. She ran up the remaining length of the gangplank and thrust herself between the two men, cursing and tearing with her nails at Lee-yen. She heard her brother shout, saw him begin to thrust the knife at Billy again and tried to push it aside. The knife jerked wildly for some seconds, then went straight into her stomach up to its hilt.

As Billy Britton told his fellow officers over grog in the ward-room that night, the woman must have been dead even before they managed to get her off the ship. And he would personally see to it that the man with the knife swung for it, even though what had happened was convenient in its way, and it would all be a great bother and bore to waste time on the death of a poor chink woman who was obviously well out of her wits.

Even those in the wardroom who regarded this attitude as a little casual said nothing; Lieutenant Billy Britton would undoubtedly become Captain or go even higher before he ended his naval career, and no one wanted highly-placed professional enemies. They were right to be cautious; and some sighed a secret sigh of relief when Vice Admiral Sir Billy Britton died of typhus at the age of fifty three while ashore in Africa, the bearer of several decorations for zealous service and bravery in action, and a renowned supporter of a Christian tract society.

*Part Five*

# 25

Tom Webster and Mr Hok sat under a striped sun umbrella at a round white table by the poolside of the Hong Kong Yacht Club as they waited for their whisky sours.

They had not yet discarded small talk. 'You come by car, Mr Webster?'

'I don't have a car, Mr Hok. I recognised yours in the car park, the large black limo with the young chauffeur, both very handsome.'

'Both very useful, Mr Webster.' Then, without a pause, Mr Hok said: 'Unusual for a news agency journalist to be so interested in what happens to a young lady and gentleman in Canton, not much copy in it, not much money, I would have thought. Now the intelligence services, I would have thought they might be more interested.'

'A journalist has many informal contacts, Mr Hok, with practically everybody. We talk with a lot of people. Matter of routine. But my interest here is personal.'

'Ha! Routine! Personal!'

'Lieutenant Britton is a friend of mine. He is now talking about throwing away his career in the navy because of a mutual acquaintance.'

Mr Hok held up a stubby hand. The chromium drinks trolley, pushed by a young Chinese with a shock of black hair standing up on his head as if he had been badly frightened, approached from the further end of the pool where Mr Hok had ordered their drinks. When Tom called him the previous day, Mr Hok had insisted on the interview taking place at the Royal Hong Kong Yacht Club rather than at his home.

'Very nice by the poolside, Mr Webster. Very good drinks trolley. Be my guest there at eleven in the morning.'

'Mr Hok, it's rather public for an interview of this sort. Apart from aspects of your business which I mentioned, I rather wanted to discuss some mutual acquaintances.'

'Yes?'

'Such as May Fong and Lieutenant Britton.' He was sure that would make Mr Hok change his mind.

'Always best to hide in open, Mr Webster. Also some nasty people about in Hong Kong, which makes it even better that we hide in open. There are many in Hong Kong whose job it is to watch others. You arrive at my home, people begin to wonder. You wave your notebook under everybody's nose at the yacht club and I sit there in full view of everybody talking to just another journalist and no one give it another thought.'

'Mr Hok, I can see we're going to get along famously.'

'Poolside Hong Kong Yacht Club, eleven in morning.'

Now Mr Hok scribbled on the bill with a gold fountain pen, lay a ten dollar note on the silver tray and switched his attention back to Tom. At other tables obviously wealthy Chinese and deeply tanned men in tropical shirts and club neckties paid them no attention. No one was using the pool, except to look at in conversational troughs. 'Had hoped you wished to discuss my new project, Mr Webster, growing bananas in the Republic and bringing them into Hong Kong. Scheme quite viable.'

Tom put down his whisky sour after a long sip. It was his turn to spring a surprise. 'Was that why you got May Fong to offer her mother money in Canton? She turned out to be party chairman of a fruit commune, I gather. Some sort of sweetener?'

Mr Hok laughed. It was a guttural, Cantonese laugh that was more like a cough. 'Is that for your news agency or your . . . contacts, Mr Webster?'

'Eventually, perhaps both, if I'm not satisfied. Did I say Lieutenant Britton is my friend?'

'And Miss Fong, of course, she is your friend.'

'I imagine she won't continue to be if your offer to her is accepted.'

'Ha! Mr Webster, you are well informed.'

Tom continued to scribble nonsense in his notebook. 'May came to me after she'd had a quarrel with Sandy Britton at the railway station when they got back yesterday. She was not pleased with him or with you, which probably explains why she came to me rather than you. They both think now that you set them up to wreck their relationship, which of course you did. May thinks that Sandy knew what he was doing, which I very much doubt. No, Mr Hok, a denial won't wash. The question is, was it money in the envelope or material which might, for instance, be of more interest to my contacts?'

Mr Hok laughed again. He had hardly touched his drink but, noticing that Tom's glass was almost empty, gesticulated to the waiter on the drinks trolley for one refill. 'Mr Webster, you can take the expatriate out of England, but you cannot take the England out of the expatriate. Isn't that a famous saying?'

'More or less. Go on.'

'I was about to say that in the East, our cultures are different.'

'Yes, I had noticed it.'

'Of course, you are a man of quick intelligence. Mr Webster, Miss Fong took with her to Canton some £20,000 in Chinese currency to be handed to her mother. In China it is not unknown for well-placed parents seeking a partner for their daughter to offer that partner money if he is not well placed, or for a well placed man seeking a woman to make a payment to her parents. In this case, the father is dead, which makes my desire to please the mother all the more understandable. My aim is always to look after those who fall within my areas of influence. Ask. Ask around. They will tell you.'

'I wish I could believe you.'

'Please yourself, Mr Webster. That is truth.'

'She still has the money. Perhaps she will let you have it back. There is one slight snag. I don't know where she is.' He gave a sanitised version of their row and her departure. 'I will do all I can to help get the money back.'

'Mr Webster, we must find her. That is more important than the money.'

'Did you know that she also had with her some £2,000 in Hong Kong dollars – money which you had handed over to her to buy her out of her employment for the four days of the Canton trip? She had not handed over the money to her . . . employers. She had that money with her in Canton, too.'

Mr Hok drank his whisky sour too quickly. 'That was foolish of her. Dangerous. A very foolish child.'

'And of course you have since seen nothing of either sum? Tell me, is Miss Fong in her present mood to be trusted?'

Mr Hok laid down his whisky glass. 'Oh, I have always found she is to be trusted, Mr Webster. Do not worry about money; money is not a problem to me. But perhaps it would not be kind to trust her or anyone else too long with such large sums of money. Not too long.'

Tom Webster said irritably: 'Why didn't you find a better way to pay Madam Shem money?'

'Such as what, Mr Webster? You cannot simply send a Chinese Communist Party official some money through the post, nor can just any person approach such a woman and hand over an envelope. Only someone like a long lost daughter can do that.'

'And had the woman accepted, it wouldn't have done your future business prospects in Canton any harm, would it?'

Mr Hok simply shrugged.

'Well, that at least is honest,' said Tom Webster. 'You used her. I see you smile. Yes, I suppose we have all used her, even Sandy and his unsuitable idealism. Where do you suppose she could be now?'

'If she is no longer with you and she is certainly not with me, then, Mr Webster, who could she be with? I would say she must be with another client. Did you know she is now interested in the Catholic religion?'

'That would be a surprise even to poor Sandy.'

'It is true. She might have sought sanctuary somewhere through that connection, though it is not very likely.'

'We must get to her before her employers get to her, wouldn't you say? That's the first priority.'

'I will make a few telephone calls concerning those quarters, but I cannot promise anything.'

'Mr Hok, we simply must get to her and get the money back before other people get to her. You must see that – even if your interest in her has been overtaken by inconvenient circumstances.'

Mr Hok gave Tom Webster a long hard look. 'My friend, what has caused you to think my interest in the lady might be at an end? It does not matter. We must make – what is the phrase? – common cause for the time being. We must find her, and quickly. Has Lieutenant Britton any ideas?'

'Thank you, Mr Hok, for your help. After what you've said I'll phone him and find out. The club must have a public phone?'

'I show you one of the more private ones, Mr Webster. Come with me. I believe in discretion. There are many Hoks in Hong Kong, some honourably in high places, but I am the most private, when I want to be. Even my own organisations do not bear my name. I shall show you how to be private.'

# 26

By eleven on Saturday morning, the walls of Tom's functional, depressingly undomestic flat pressed intolerably in on Sandy. He had not wanted to come to Tom's flat to see if May was there – he was frightened of what he might find – but he had come.

Once his unwanted guest had satisfied himself that May had gone in a huff, Tom, who had declined to elaborate further, had suggested he go back to the ship and stay there. 'I'll let you know anything there is to know, Sandy, Scouts honour. You'll be safer on the ship from every point of view.'

'Nice of you to be concerned about my safety, but I'd like to stay. If anything happens, I'd like to be among the first to hear it. She may be in trouble.'

'She's in trouble all right, that much we can be sure of. We don't know how many thousand dollars she has on her but we do know none of it is hers. The people she works for tend to resent that sort of thing.'

'I've decided. I'll chuck the navy, I'll ask her to marry me and take her away from here. There's nothing any of you can do to stop me.'

'Except the navy can put you in irons or whatever they do now for desertion. Sandy, take three bloody aspirin and lie down.'

'I'm quite serious.'

'That's why I'm suggesting you take three aspirin and lie down. She doesn't want to know you.'

'Because of all the things you lot have done to her.'

'You lot? Include yourself, old son. I had no trouble before and neither did she. Maybe she'd have shacked up with Hok and maybe she wouldn't have. Things worked, until you showed up with a prick two feet long and a boy scout sense of honour. They don't run happily in tandem, old son, they can cause big trouble, or haven't you noticed yet?'

'Tom, sometimes I find your crudity pretty difficult to take.'

'Sometimes I find your juvenility impossible to take. Oh, stop here if you want to, at least I can keep an eye on you and maybe get you to count up to ten. And you'd better turn in early, you look like shit.'

This conversation and the events that had led up to it had been rolling around in his guts like bad indigestion all night. The bed in Tom's almost bare guest bedroom pressed on his bones as if it had concrete in it, and he had hardly slept a wink. Tom had found him sitting on the lavatory bowl in the bathroom with the door still open at half past three in the morning.

'What the hell are you doing?'

'I can't sleep. I tried not to disturb you.'

'You were talking to yourself. For the last few minutes you've been shouting about May, me and Hok. Get back to bed, for heaven's sake. Get a grip on yourself. We may need to be at our best to respond to what our friend Mr Hok tells us.'

'If he'll tell us a thing. Anyway, what's he know? He wasn't there in Canton. That's where it all happened, that's the key. It's all hopeless.'

'Some contacts of mine think he may have been represented. Does that ring any bells? Mr Hok must have many friends in the business and banking world here, but so do I.'

'Sam Browne! I thought there was something odd about him and his whole attitude. I just thought he had a personality problem, as we say in the navy.'

'Yes, well, before I excite you further, you'd better get back to bed and try to get some shuteye. Don't despair, that's the main thing, but don't build up any rosy pictures, either.'

'Tom, you don't think I'm going mad, do you?'

'Show me a man who says he's sane and I'll show you a liar.'

'No, seriously.'

'Of course you're not going mad. Just take it easy, and don't do anything terminally silly, that's all.'

Tom had left some wheat and bran flakes in two bowls on the breakfast bar in the narrow kitchen, but Sandy couldn't fancy any of his. He simply sat there in his pyjamas – he was lucky he had them with him from the Canton trip – and stared out of the window towards the harbour as Tom wittered on about the questions he was going to ask Mr Hok and how he was not going to be put off whatever Mr Hok said by way of evasion.

'Cheerio, Tom,' he said with relief, as his grudging host disappeared through the front door of the flat in grey trousers, blue striped short-sleeved shirt and green striped tie that looked vaguely as if it might be academic or regimental.

By the time Tom was due to meet Mr Hok, Sandy had come to the conclusion that his friend was wasting his time, that the last thing Mr Hok would do was help a known friend of his in any way at all, and that he would be better employed looking for her on his own.

He had been walking the streets for no more than half an hour when something Tom had said when he had asked him hours ago where he thought May might possibly have sought sanctuary after she had left his flat, and Tom had replied, with his usual facetiousness, something like, 'Not in a convent taking holy vows, we may be sure!'

Why so sure? She had once told him, the first time they had been together, that she was interested in the Catholic religion, and he had thought it was just something she said because she thought that was the type of thing he might want to hear, though in fact he had little interest in religion of any kind. Even if it wasn't a lead, at least it would enable him to get out of this depressing apartment and do something.

Sandy set off in the direction of the Convent of the Blessed Virgin. He could have taken a cab and got there in a fraction of the time, but the suspicion that he might find absolutely nothing when he got there persuaded him to put off that unwelcome discovery as long as possible by walking. It was a good two miles, and for the last half mile, he wondered what he would do when he got there. Knock at the door and ask them if they had a girl hiding there? They might well fling him out. He should have stayed in Tom's apartment until he had heard in full what Mr Hok had to say.

Sandy did not need to knock at the door. As he approached, he saw that in front of the Convent of the Blessed Virgin was a playground on which girls of various ages played or sat around reading in the shade of trees. He had not known the convent was also a school. Between him on the wide pavement and the playground was a tall black cast iron fence with gilt decoration. Through this he could see not only the girls but also May as she stalked out of the main doors as if in a hurry, looking straight ahead.

Surely it was May this time, or was he really going mad? Several times since they had returned from Canton he had thought a girl was May, only to find on closer inspection that she was really not like May at all.

He followed her with his eyes as she walked through the playground towards the gate. She saw him as she was halfway to the gate. He was sure she recognised him.

She turned, and quickly walked back to the main doors of the convent. As she disappeared behind them, Sandy was left with the smile still frozen on his face.

# 27

May Fong left the Convent of the Blessed Virgin much more abruptly than usual. Always, for the past three years, she had seen Sister Lai Yen every week. Usually, after passing over the money, she liked to stay long enough for a cup of sweet tea, long discussions about the Christian God – they appeared to have only one – and short discussions about herself which May Fong usually ended by looking hard at her watch.

This time Sister Lai Yen had first talked very enthusiastically about the Messiaen and Mozart public concert at the convent and then told her, after she had clapped her hands and said she had known all along that her sister was a genius, that she must not be unrealistic. 'We know that your sister is a fine violinist for a child, a very fine one indeed. But not all prodigies develop into adult professional performers, you know, some fall by the wayside.'

'She will not fall by the wayside. I know. You say she could have extra lessons from a professional, I pay for those.'

'They would be very expensive indeed, my child. The convent has only once arranged it in the twenty years I have been here. I do not think you could afford it.'

'I pay.'

'I mean very expensive. You must trust what I say, May Fong. How long have you been coming here?'

'Every week for three years. Do I ever miss bringing you money to help the convent? Do I ever bring you less?'

'Three years – well, you should trust me, May Fong. Wait and see how she develops. Then it will be time to decide if she warrants further professional training.'

'One day she play in the Royal Festival Hall, London, the Royal Albert Hall, London, and here in Hong Kong. She never go back to China, no – not as good as Hong Kong. Suppose I marry rich old man and then have enough money?'

To her great irritation. Sister Lai Yen laughed. 'Christianity teaches that marriages are made in heaven, child, not for that sort of convenience.'

'Even if I did it for something good?'

'It would be a great wrong, both to yourself and to whoever you would be marrying. And to your sister too, for that matter – if you were your sister, would you wish to know that your profession as a musician rested on a sacrifice of that sort?'

'Not much of sacrifice. At present I get money by – '

'I don't want to know, May Fong. We don't want to know. We never have, not unless you want to have proper confession.'

She had stormed out, the twenty thousand dollars that was supposed to buy her out for four days in Canton left in the hand of Sister Lai Yen, the envelope containing the money Mr Hok had tried to get her to pass to her mother still in her pocket.

'I'm afraid it would take more than twenty thousand dollars to cover a professional's tuition. May Fong.'

'Then I bring you more.'

'May, we will put this towards her normal education and living expenses . . . '

Stupid cow! Quite as bad as any of these European gweilos.

She forced herself to smile and wave cheerfully to her sister, playing happily in the playground in front of the convent, as she walked back towards the road. Then she turned. Sandy Britton was watching her through the railings no more than a hundred metres away.

She turned away, choking for breath as if someone, somewhere was choking the life out of her. She quickly walked back into the convent.

# 28

While he was waiting for her to come out again, Sandy looked around the playground. Some of the Chinese girls were incredibly pretty in their pigtails, others were solemn but equally touching in their spectacles. All wore grey shirts and skirts.

Under one of the trees, on her own, sat by far the prettiest girl in the playground. She was sitting cross-legged on the ground, reading a bulky book and seemingly oblivious of all around her. Her ivory face was long for a Chinese.

At first, the resemblance was so uncanny that Sandy thought it could be May herself. Then the implication hit him like a punch in the stomach. There was a younger sister after all, and the girl he was watching was her. Why else should May be visiting a convent, and showing every sign of knowing her way about? Perhaps she had taken sanctuary there last night, perhaps she hadn't; but it was plain that May was keeping an eye on her younger sister, perhaps devoting some or nearly all of her tainted earnings to the education and welfare of this beautiful child.

Child? It was difficult to tell ages where the Chinese were concerned, but she could be fifteen, though fourteen was more likely.

Sandy walked into the playground. Some of the girls skipping near the gate looked at him curiously, others ignored him. A highly coloured ball landed near his feet. He stopped to pick it up and throw it to the group of girls near the convent door. They laughed and shouted something in Cantonese and when he shouted back, 'You're welcome,' one of the older girls in the group said something else in Cantonese and the whole group began to giggle.

Sandy walked over to the girl reading under the tree. At first she did not see him. How tenderly beautiful she was, like May herself must have been at her age: even more beautiful, perhaps. At last, as his shadow fell on her, she looked up.

'Are you May Fong's sister?' he asked. It sounded stupid, but what else was he to say?

'Who are you, please?' said the girl cautiously. Her voice was lighter than May's, with the more sing-song inflection of Chinese who hadn't had to adapt greatly to Western ears.

'A friend of May's.'

'She has many friends. Yes, I am her sister.'

'I'm a close friend. What are you reading?'

She held up the book so he could see the cover.

'Ah! Bunyan's *Pilgrim's Progress*. I had to read that at school too. I found it a bit heavy, I remember.'

'Is a rattling good story if you understand it properly,' she said in solemn tones, inadequately hiding a smile. 'Perhaps your teachers were not overly perceptive. The nuns explain it to us very well.'

It was Sandy's turn to hide a smile. That May devoted herself to caring for this lovely young creature assured him that his feelings for May had not been a mistake, they had been bang-on. He must talk to her, he must make her believe he was sincere.

Sandy was not usually greatly at ease in the presence of younger people. He began to chat with May's young sister as if they had known one another for years.

# 29

Sister Lai Yen was still standing in the corridor near the door when May returned.

'My child, what is it? You look as if you have seen a ghost.'

'A ghost, yes. How long could my sister have professional violin tuition if I were to pay you fifty thousand dollars?'

'Where would you possibly get fifty thousand dollars?'

'Is no matter.'

'Well, about a year's tuition, perhaps.'

May thrust the envelope into her hands. 'You take this, please. You can count it. Fifty thousand dollars.'

'May, where did you get this money? Did you get it honestly?'

'You count it, please.'

'May, that isn't the point. If you say there's fifty thousand dollars there, I'm sure there is. But did you come by it honestly?'

'You never ask me questions before.'

'Because the sums of money were less, such as you could have earned yourself. Even the twenty thousand dollars you brought today could have been come by honestly. But another fifty thousand . . .'

'Was gift to my mother, instead her daughter get it, okay?'

'No, not quite, how could – '

May was already walking towards the door.

# 30

Sandy was laughing with the young girl over something Mr Valiant For Truth had said in *The Pilgrim's Progress* when he saw that he had lost the girl's attention. She was looking at something behind him. The next moment May seized him by his left arm and swung him round to face her.

'You leave her alone!'

'May! How wonderful to see you! We must talk. I have something very important to say to you.'

'You take your hands off her!'

'What's the matter? I always knew you were a saint through and through. I told Tom more than once.'

'You get away from her! Her as well? No!'

'May, everything's all right, I'm going to leave the navy and be here with you! We'll manage somehow.'

May's speech became a maddened scream. 'You stupid Englishman! You fuck me, now you want to fuck her?'

The playground had become deathly quiet apart from her screams.

'May, you don't understand . . .'

'You go and leave us! We do not want you here! We manage well without you! Go! Filth!'

He turned to her sister. 'We were only laughing about *The Pilgrim's Progress*, weren't we?'

'You leave her alone, English filth! Keep away from her!'

He began to raise both his hands to pacify the hysterical May. Only this prevented the little knife May had concealed in her hand from going into his chest. It landed in his shoulder instead.

It felt like a red hot needle. He gaped silently in surprise as May ran out of the gate and into the street. His hand to his bleeding shoulder, he stumbled after her.

'May! You've got it all wrong! May! Please!'

She was no more fifty paces ahead of him in the street when the young Chinese man in the light blue suit came out of a doorway behind her immediately she had passed it, the shiny meat cleaver already in his hand.

The first blow cut deep into the back of her neck and swung her round. The second cut into her throat and killed her.

Sandy stopped only ten paces from the young Chinese, who had the bloodied meat cleaver still raised. For an eternity lasting a few seconds, they stared into one another's eyes. Sandy stood rooted to the spot, sure he was a dead man. Then the man in the light blue suit tucked the cleaver inside his jacket and calmly walked away into a side street.

Sandy fell to his knees and tried to cradle May's lifeless body in his arms, his tears uniting with the blood on her throat and face. He wished he were a dead man.

# 31

In the long grey years that followed, Sandy Britton often asked himself just what he had done that was so very wrong, and what he could have done instead. An answer might have eased the burden of the bewilderment and guilt. But he couldn't, ever, come up with a satisfactory answer.

Was it wrong that, unlike men who used women as objects, he had felt and behaved very differently to one of them? Was it wrong that she had been Chinese instead of English, with yellow skin instead of white, and had lived in Hong Kong rather than Harrogate or Hendon? Was it wrong of him to try to put her in touch with her long-lost mother? How could that have been wrong?

But she was dead, and dead because neither Mr Hok with his money nor he with his love had been able to defend her. Sometimes he relived those last wonderful and horrible days in the hope of making sense of them, but he never did. Had the Chinese man in the light blue suit who had tried to snatch her handbag in Canton been the same as the one with the cleaver in Hong Kong, or was only the suit similar? When she had turned back into the convent on her last day on earth, was it himself she had seen or the blue-suited man, or both?

And a more dreadful thought: was it entirely her feelings for him which had tempted her to try to get away from her trade and the men behind it, and so sealed her fate? An even more dreadful thought: was spotting him outside the convent that last day the moment she had decided she would pass over all the money to the sisters, knowing that she was finished? And still more dreadful: had he, by going to the convent, unwittingly guided the man with the cleaver directly to her?

These thoughts went round and round in his mind while, on the surface, his professional life progressed as if little or nothing had happened to him. He was not to be allowed even the comfort of madness. But if his stiff upper lip outwardly held, he was unable to explain the sense of guilt that dogged him, however easy it was to explain the sense of loss. If he had had a human fault in the whole tragic business, what was it? Was it a fault that, when he was trying to find May that last time, he had found and liked the younger sister who reminded him so much of her? Was it his fault that May had gone wildly out of control, and that the men behind the bar girl traffic were almost certainly gangs who had decided to make an example of her rebellion and also shut her mouth for ever? Was it his fault that he had ignored the advice of both Tom and the Captain, albeit oblique, to forget her? How could loving her far too much to take that advice be a fault?

It seemed to Sandy, in the long empty years, as if the only 'fault' he could trace to himself was that he had tried to behave in a human way to another human being when obviously the unwritten rules had been quite different. A lot of men who never made that mistake seemed to cause less trouble and suffering to themselves and others than he had done. It affected his confidence not only in his relations with women, but also in his human judgment. When you opened yourself up to human feeling you got hurt and, worse, you hurt others. It was best to do everything strictly by the book.

For many years, this thought was seldom far from his increasingly formal and detached mind. He drummed it into younger officers. A cynic like Tom Webster, had he still been around, might have said he was simply another victim of a now-fallen British Empire; that, but for that empire, he and May might have met as equals and things would have been all right between them. But he couldn't believe that – too simple, and a bit subversive.

Nor could he foresee the future, and derided those who tried. Had he been told beforehand that in the year 2041 a distant cousin's son, Lieutenant Commander Sammy Britton, would marry in Hong Kong Miss May Kuen Fong, a daughter of the chairman of the Chinese Trade Administration and one of Hong Kong's finest amateur violinists, who did not know her mother's late older sister had been a bar girl; and that this wedding would be one of the territory's smartest social events of the year, he would have called the prediction wildly imaginative – his favourite term of disapproval.

Sometimes he had a vague, worrying and quite irrational feeling that he was being punished for something, but he kept it to himself; if you weren't careful that sort of thing could lead to religious mania or something of that kind; and that could be damned embarrassing.

Professionally, he lived down his youthful past and went smoothly through the ranks of Lieutenant, Lieutenant Commander, Commander and finally Captain – one of the few unmarried Captains in the Royal Navy of the twenty-first century, and one who could therefore be sent without warning or domestic recriminations to any ship or shore establishment, a great asset to the Royal Navy.

His mild youthful indiscretion in taking up to the Chinese mainland on a stupid jaunt some Hong Kong bar girl who later got herself killed was soon buried deep and unregarded in his personal file. The Royal Navy, he knew, prided itself on dealing with a man as he was today, not as he had been in the days of his youthful errors. Many a randy young ass, he had been told, had made good.

Sandy never saw Tom Webster again, ignoring the Christmas cards that Tom sent for many years until he died, still in Hong Kong, in mysterious circumstances. Sandy was amusedly observed by curious younger officers to make a point of hardly leaving the ship when it put into Chinese-controlled Hong Kong. Most of them put it down to a typically pernickety, strait-laced fear of the remotest possibility of an international incident involving himself.

He left the Royal Navy early for health reasons after having a mild stroke, and the younger men said I-told-you-so. He retired to a Dorset cottage where, at his death at seventy-three, he was found to have few possessions of any great value, but a huge collection of books on the Royal Navy and the British Empire. There was also an artistically indifferent etching, dated the previous year, of a Chinese girl.

The disappointed pink-cheeked young auctioneer, collating the household effects for the sale, and trying desperately to impress his beautiful girl assistant, said in a superior sarcastic tone that it must have been bought because it reminded the old buffer of somebody.